Praise for Tim Hall's *Half Empty*:

"A splendid trip into the modern psychosis of the New York City male."

Bully Magazine

"His writing snaps like a fallen power line. Born ranters can sometimes pull off enviable fiction."

Zine World

"His characters are vivid—especially Dennis, a mixture of absurd macho posturing and deflated self-loathing, with an attitude towards the opposite sex that veers between gushing sentimentality and crass sexual opportunism."

Kirkus Discoveries

"Another admirable effort, and a much more traditionally satisfying narrative. It's a story in the classic confused-young-man genre of Goethe's suicidal aesthete and Salinger's irritable preppie."

LitKicks.com

"[A] sexy and funny book that reflects the lives of normal people and also gives us something back. Highly recommended."

Fifteen Project

"An awesome local novel."

Mediadiet.net

By TIM HALL

You Can't Kiss A Child With Apocalypse (1998)
The Bloodsucker Trilogy (1999)
Comfy Assumptions (2001)
Club It Up (2001)
Scumsquat Farewell (2002)
Poopstain (2002)
Mean Time Before Failure (2002)
Half Empty (2004)

TRIUMPH
OF THE
WON'T

TIM HALL

Undie Press
Jersey City

To Kirk

THANKS!

Tim Hall
10/11/08

TRIUMPH OF THE WON'T

Published by Undie Press
undiepress@mac.com
www.undiepress.com

ISBN: 0-976-34603-6

First Printing: June 2006

Some of these stories first appeared in *The New York Hangover,
NY Press, Chicago Reader, Go Metric, Bullymag.com, Dogmatika, Slush
Pile*, and *BIGnews*

for Dean Haspiel

I do not really care how the naturalists maltreat language, but I do strenuously object to the earthiness of their ideas. They have made our literature the incarnation of materialism—and they glorify the democracy of art!

—J.K. Huysmans

TRIUMPH OF THE WON'T

Keeping It Real With Kid Beluga

Kid was pacing the floor, chain-smoking budget cigarettes.

"Dude, this is so awesome! We're gonna be huge!"

"I hope so."

Jack Martin sat in a chair by the window. Jack was going to publish Kid's second book of poems, *Straight Outta Steeltown*. Jack had found Kid's first book in a forgotten corner of a local bookstore and thought it was one of the strongest collections he had ever read. It had been published by a small print-on-demand house, somewhere in the Midwest. Jack had gotten Kid's email address from the publisher and written to him, and that's when Kid sent him the new work, asking Jack if he'd publish it. The new collection was even better than the first one, and Jack had talked it over with Dolly and she agreed.

Kid ran to the computer and punched some keys.

"Holy shit, I got ten more hits in the past half hour!"

Kid was checking his website again. There was a free hit counter at the bottom of the home page and Kid checked it several times an hour, hoping for more visitors.

11

"Kid," Jack said, "Those aren't hits."

"What are you talking about? Of course they are!"

"What I mean is, the number keeps going up because you keep checking every few minutes. Those ten visits are from you."

"No they're not! No way!"

Jack walked over to the computer and took the mouse. He scrolled down to the bottom of the page.

"Look. Here's your counter, right? What does it say?"

"678."

"Okay. Now I'm going to hit the page reload button. What does it say now?"

"679."

"Exactly."

"But that doesn't mean anything! Somebody could have come to the site during that time!"

Jack started hitting the reload button over and over.

"See? Look at it now: 682...683...684...."

"All right! Stop it!"

"What's the matter?"

"You're messing up my *statistics*! I have to know how many *hits* I'm getting and I don't want you screwing it up!"

Kid grabbed the mouse from Jack and clicked.

"Damn! Now it says 685!"

It was always a danger with these underground types. Jack had seen it before. They could play it very cool until something started to happen, then most of them went nuts. He and Kid had spoken by phone and written many emails over the months, but it wasn't until Kid took the bus to Jersey City from Steeltown that he started talking about blogs and hits and the rest of it.

Kid's blog was called *Dis Is How Da Lit Game Be Played.* Jack had tried reading it once. It was written in a gangster-rap style,

12

full of *yo* and *word* and nonsensical talk about *keepin' it real.* Jack thought it was a joke at first, but Kid was serious. He had started the blog with the help of another blogger named Chigger Lee. Chigger had done an interview with Kid on his site, *The Saddest Blog in the World.* Like Kid, Chigger was young and a little too preoccupied with himself. He wrote short, clipped lines using all lowercase letters, usually about the state of his soul:

i am so sad
i do not know why i am sad
but i am
i guess being sad makes me happy
which is kind of funny if you think about it
but then again
maybe not

It was cute at first, harmless, but then Chigger caught the attention of some of the bigger literary bloggers, who linked to him, and when he saw his hit counter jump it had gone to his head. Chigger decided that he had something to say, which is a dangerous thing for anybody with unlimited Internet access and free publishing software. Then it wasn't cute any more. Chigger had the same narrow, shitty little philosophies and prejudices that most people lost after freshman year. His philosophy revolved around the assertion that there was no such thing as good or bad, because everything was based on *feelings*, and if you didn't *feel* Hitler was a bad guy then that meant that nobody else could claim that he was, because that would negate your *feelings*, and feelings were all that really mattered.

Kid clicked again.

"Shit! I forgot. What was the last number?"

13

"Give it a rest," Jack said.

"Dude, no way! I think Bookslob is about to link to my post about him. I want to see how many people click to my site!"

"You wrote about Bookslob?"

"Yeah! I called him a fucking dick!"

"For God's sake, why?"

"Why do you think? So he would link to me! Ha ha! Hey, haven't you been reading my blog?"

"I've been busy."

"I also attacked Mishkin in a recent post. Mishkin is such a fucking asshole!"

"I can't argue with that," Jack said.

"If he attacks me on his blog you gotta defend me!"

"Why don't you defend yourself?"

"Because I don't wanna deal with that asshole!"

"Then why did you attack him?"

"Because that's how it's done, man! That's how the lit game is played! It's fucking awesome, dude!"

Nine months, Jack thought. For nine months Kid Beluga had seemed like a smart, normal kid. He had a bit of a rough upbringing but so did lots of people. And he had talent, but that wasn't enough either. That's why most writers failed; they spent so much time inside their own heads that when the time came to shine they couldn't come to terms with their own suppressed desires. They had thin skins, or faulty insulation, and burned up on entry.

Kid went back to the computer.

"Why do you care how many visitors your blog gets?" Jack asked.

"Because I wanna blow up big! My book's gonna be huge! Chigger says he got like two thousand hits when Jolly Bookworm linked to him! And Bookwhore gets something like 7,000 hits a day!"

Kid didn't understand the difference between hits, visitors, and unique visitors. Jack didn't feel like explaining it to him. He felt the whole topic might make him sick at any moment. Kid checked his little digital counter like a child standing at the refrigerator door, yanking it open with the hope that he might catch the light when it's off.

"Are you sure that's the best way to get attention?" Jack asked.

"What do you mean?"

"I mean, these blogs are all voluntary. They don't *have* to link to you, and why would they want to if you call them assholes?"

"No way, dude, they're gonna link to me, totally! You don't understand how it works!"

"Never attack anybody who buys ink by the barrel," Jack said.

"What are you talking about? This is the *Internet*, man, there ain't no ink! Ha ha! That's the stupidest thing I've ever heard!"

"Forget it. What I mean is...why?"

"Because I want a fucking swimming pool! In 20 years I want to be chilling by the pool in my big-ass crib, drinking with a bunch of hotties!"

Jack forced a smile and didn't answer. *Wholesaler, 55 percent. Distributor, another 15.* Then there were postage, envelopes, returns, damage to think about.

"Are we gonna have distribution in England?"

"I don't know yet. Not right away. I'm still working on it."

"You know Fidel Goldberg? He runs Suburban Fuckface Press."

"Sounds familiar."

15

"He says they have distribution in England. What's my royalty again?"

"I don't know yet. Depends on print run, advance, cover price. It's based on a percentage; there's still a lot we have to figure out."

"Fidel says all his writers get a buck-fifty a book."

"So why don't you publish with Fidel?"

"Because he's print-on-demand! Fuck POD! My last publisher was POD and he fucking sucked! You're doing it old school, and that's what I like!"

"So why do you keep comparing me to him?"

Kid's face dropped.

"Oh." His voice became a whisper. "I'm real sorry."

Jack rubbed his head. *Mailing lists. Direct marketing. Advertising. Press releases. Postcards.* So much to keep track of, so many decisions. And with such a small budget it was hard to figure out the best moves and easy to make the wrong ones. Not to mention reviews, letters to the editor, readings, open bars, associations, clubs, dues, newsletters, forums, fairs, feuds. And while he figured it out there were a thousand others with more experience all fighting for the same few inches of shelf space. It was madness.

"You've got a great view of the city," Kid said.

"Thanks."

"Dude, do you know where I can get a Che Guevara T-Shirt? I really want one of those."

"For yourself?"

"Yeah! Maybe I'll get one for Snookie too. She'd like that."

"I don't know," Jack said. "St. Mark's Place, probably."

"Would you take me down there so I could look?"

"Sure, we'll go tomorrow."

"Dude, if we find them you should totally get one too!"

"Why would I want that bastard's face on my chest?"

Kid looked wounded.

"What are you talking about? Che was a fucking revolutionary, man, he fought against Capitalist oppression!"

"He was a dog and a coward. He spent most of his time shooting rivals in the back. When the real heat came he ran to the hills. Some hero."

Jack immediately regretted saying it. Not because it wasn't true, but because it didn't matter. He was tired of arguing with suburban socialists. Kid was a fine writer, but Jack had no more patience for the *petite Marxoisie* and their shitty politics.

"Dude, I can't believe you're saying that..."

"You're right, it doesn't matter," Jack said.

"Do you think this country is fair? Do you think we live in a just society?"

"Didn't you tell me you live rent-free, in a house your girlfriend's parents gave her?"

"What does that have to do with anything?"

"Forget it," Jack said. "Look, I'm here to talk books, not politics. Are you going to want videos on the site too?"

"Totally! Of course! And podcasts! Remember we talked about podcasts!"

"I remember."

Jack looked out the windows. In the distance, the hazy Manhattan skyline seemed to float on top of the trees of the Jersey City Heights. There were birds bathing in the old reservoir off Summit Avenue. Down below, on Route 139, souped-up economy cars painted in the bright enamels of a grocery store checkout girl's fingernails were being driven by scowling youths with military haircuts.

It was a late summer afternoon, heavy with dying promise. Kid Beluga still paced, smoking his budget cigarettes, but with a difference. The pacing now felt to Jack like a measurement, as if Kid were trying to gauge just how big the divide between them was: the east coast publisher with the view of Manhattan, and the unemployed young writer struggling in a former steel town in the middle of nowhere. At least that was how Kid portrayed it in his work. The truth was never so simple.

A few things kept nagging at him. Like how Kid was living, for one. In the book there were a lot of raw, powerful poems about growing up poor white trash in Steeltown, but a number of things didn't add up. Kid didn't work; he lived rent-free. They got by on what his girlfriend earned. Another time Kid had bragged that his parents earned almost 80 thousand a year between them when he was growing up. There was nothing wrong with any of that, but to hear Kid tell it he was forever being kept down by the invisible boot of The Man. Jack had grown up with four siblings and a single mom who worked for minimum wage. Kid might have grown up white trash, but he sure as hell wasn't poor. Che Guevara could suck a dick.

"You've got a real nice place here," Kid said softly. His voice was still a whisper, but high and feminine now, almost like a taunt.

Mortgage, Jack thought. Taxes. Insurance.

"Thanks. It's a stretch, but with Dolly's new job we're doing okay."

"You've got a real nice view, a doorman and everything."

Maintenance. Fees. Assessments. Monthly subway passes. Parking. Tolls.

"We got lucky. We couldn't afford anyplace else. This is the last undiscovered neighborhood that's so close to the city. It reminds me of Williamsburg back in the early 90s. A little scummy, but not too bad."

"What's Brooklyn like?"

"It's no good any more. It's all become fabulous, even the bad parts. It's a shame, really. It used to be nice. Now it makes my teeth hurt. When I walk around Park Slope or Smith Street I have trouble breathing. I can't explain it."

"Dude, fuck Brooklyn! You gotta stay ghetto, like 50 Cent! I wanna be like him, a gangsta rapper in the poetry world! I'm gonna have mad skills in the lit game!"

"Maybe we could make a T-shirt of you, wearing a beret with a star. We'll call you Kid Guevara."

"Ha ha ha! Dude, that would be amazing! Are you serious? Can we really do that?"

"I don't know," Jack said. "It would be expensive."

"Who cares? It'll be totally worth it!"

Jack looked at his watch. He wondered when Dolly would be getting home. He hoped she would remember to stop at the cash machine, so they could pay for Kid's bus ticket back. One more day, he thought. Eighty thousand a year is a lot of money, even in Jersey City. In a place like Steeltown it would be a small fortune. He smiled. Forget 50 Cent; maybe they would call Kid *80 Grand* instead. Jack smiled, then stopped himself. Envy was a luxury only the lazy could afford.

Cocaine

Ernie got the stuff from a fat Jewish kid who had a connection in the Bronx. Larry, that was the Jewish kid's name, had a dirty red afro and listened to Grateful Dead bootlegs while he weighed it out. There was a slow, underwater look to all his movements, which was strange considering how much of the product he was sampling.

It wasn't supposed to be like this at the University of Chicago. I had pictured cardigan sweaters, and long walks through autumnal paths with intense, bookish women. I had imagined deep philosophical discussions with avuncular, bearded professors in shabby tweeds and Birkenstocks. What I'd gotten instead was a fat drug dealer, sweating under a solitary bulb while he cut cocaine off a kilo brick. I had always thought drugs were fun, until I started selling them.

It was the school's fault, I kept telling myself. If only they hadn't lured me to their big prestigious university with all those scholarships and financial aid, only to tell me the summer before my sophomore year they were cutting my aid by three thousand dollars. When I'd applied I was homeless, living in a friend's basement. All I had were the savings from a summer job and a small settlement from an accident I'd had as a kid, both of which had already been figured in. I'd argued with the financial aid office, written letters and reminded them that I was on the Dean's List and that this amounted to academic bait-and-switch. In the end they restored some of my aid, but it didn't matter much. I was still screwed.

It started simply enough. Ernie and I were doing lines one night and I mentioned my financial troubles. He said that the stuff he got was so pure that if I bought an eightball I could cut half of it back up to an eighth, sell it for a nice profit and still get a numb nose out of the deal. It sounded good, so I agreed. Ernie fronted me the drugs and that weekend I sold the eightball to a freshman at a Bangles concert. Even after paying Ernie back I had made a nice profit, something like a hundred dollars for two minutes of work. I was in business.

From there, it was easy. If I needed books, or new tubes for my guitar amp, I sold a few grams, made my profit, and still had enough left over to keep me wired through the weekend. Before long Ernie and I were known for having the best drugs on campus. We were successful because we weren't greedy. We only stepped on the blow 20 or 30 percent, where it could have easily withstood twice that. Sometimes we didn't cut it at all, and simply wrapped up a giant rock for some lucky person to dive into.

I had rules. First, I never carried more than a gram or two on me at any time, with the idea that if I ever got busted I could convince the cops that it wasn't intended for resale. Also, I never sold directly to strangers. When people I didn't know wanted to score I always denied being a dealer but told them that I knew somebody, and that in fact I was hoping to score some too, and that if we pooled our money I could probably get us a better deal. I'd take their money and run off, pull the stuff from my sock or money belt or wherever, and come back with two triangular envelopes carefully cut from the glossy pages of porno magazines and folded expertly so that a large breast or spread vagina was prominently featured. I'd let the buyer choose which one he or she wanted and then take the other. I never, under any circumstances, partied with the customers. As soon as the deal was done, so was I.

Ernie was more open about it. On the weekend there would be a line of eager students fidgeting outside his bedroom door. He made a lot more money than I did, but I thought he was crazy for being so obvious.

Around this time I began dating a girl from the local high school, a 16-year-old brick shithouse named Gretchen, who smoked a pipe—a real pipe, with tobacco—and was legally independent from her parents. Gretchen lived in a big apartment with another teenager, a lissome bisexual named Willow. Gretchen was a waitress at a local diner and used to throw her tips under the bed. She lifted the sheet one day and showed me. It was an enormous pile, obscene. There must have been a few thousand dollars, all in coins and singles. I asked her why she just left it there and Gretchen shrugged and said she had no time to count small bills or change.

Gretchen loved her cocaine, and had her own source, which was nice: it meant that she wasn't just using me for my drugs. I did lines off her tits, her ass, and she'd sprinkle a little on my balls and lick it off, and then we'd fuck in a sweaty stupor for hours. I once even rubbed a little on her asshole because she wanted it up the pooper, but the coke made the head of my cock numb and I began to lose the erection, and we finally gave

22

up after a few minutes of trying to stuff my flaccid member up her toilet.

Sometimes when I left her place I'd take some money from under the bed. It was never much—two or nine dollars—but I pretended I was being paid for sex and that turned me on. Then Ernie began dating Willow, and we'd all party together, but we could never achieve our true goal, which was to get the two of them together and have one big orgy. We'd all sit around, doing lines and drinking and smoking, and at some point Willow would shimmer off to her room without a word and after 20 minutes or so Ernie would get up and shrug and follow her in there. As soon as they would leave Gretchen would pull open her shirt and lean back, and I'd grab the baggy and straw and go to work on those tits.

Gretchen was bold. One night she took me to a local Thai restaurant, and as soon as we sat down she stood her menu up like a screen and cut lines on the plate and did them right there. I was so freaked out that I broke it off with her a few days later. Apart from drugs and sex there wasn't a whole lot for us to do or talk about, anyway. She took the news well, and we even had one last fling on her old iron bed, but I didn't take any money that time.

It was bad enough knowing that I was contributing to the moral and physical decline of my fellow students, but when I finally stopped dealing it was because of The Look. When they know you're selling drugs, people look at you differently. It's instantaneous and irrevocable. I knew that my peers, my respected academic colleagues, thought I was a scumbag. And they were probably right.

Ernie had no such problems; he continued to deal, but in a more low-key way. I began to stay in more, and do more drugs. I

23

was mixing crank with my cocaine, and even came up with a name for it: croke. I would be so hungover in the mornings that I would have to do a line to make my 8:30 Spanish class.

A few weeks before the end of the school year I woke up in my room and looked around. There were baggies, bottles and cigarette butts everywhere. The girl snoring next to me was some pig from Wisconsin, a plump little thing who had vacuumed plenty of my drugs up her snout the night before but wouldn't let me fuck her. She kept saying things like "sex is dirty, sex is disgusting," while I had four fingers up her twat and one of her nipples in my mouth. I knew right then that I wouldn't be coming back, that my career at Chicago was over. Financially, I was worse off than before. I had used my drug proceeds to pay some of my tuition bill but my savings were all gone, and I had no job lined up, no plans, nothing to look forward to.

I also knew that I wouldn't be doing any more cocaine for a long, long time.

I woke the pig up with my elbow, and she snorted.

"What day is it?" I asked her.

"Saturday," she mumbled.

"Not the day of the week," I snapped, "the month. What's the date?"

"Um, May 12, I think. Why?"

"It's my birthday," I said.

Big Marie

The acid was kicking in when Big Marie came out of the bathroom dressed only in a pink bath towel. She walked to the bedroom and shut the door. There was a line already.

I had been holding the guitar for a while, I was the only one who could play. The strings were shimmering laser beams of gold jelly, and I'd finally found a song that everybody could sing along to.

We are one person,
We are two alone

The first guy went in. We didn't hear anything. When he came out a little while later he was looking like he invented it. The next one went in.

We are three together
We are for each other....

It went on like that for a while. The door opened, the door closed. When it was open there was nothing but inky blackness, but I could see roiling waves of pink perfumed sex billowing out of the room—or the rat-stinking piss of toothless hooker alleys, depending on where my head was at. But I was having a good time. The girl sitting across from me was a skintight Greek goddess, ripped Levi's showing a passionate knee, the wood paneling behind her malachite hair pulsing alive with chemical sap.

"I'll get you beers if you'll keep playing," she said.

Big Marie came out and announced she was taking a break. The group at the door murmured dejectedly. She went to the fridge, got a beer, and wandered in and out of rooms, nothing on but the pink towel, which looked more like a dishrag on her. The six of us in the circle in the corner were heavy into a new song:

Be on my side
I'll be on your side

Marie came over and stood next to me.

"I thought you were gonna come in! You said you and your friend there were going to play cards on my back." She was talking about Satish, who was still a virgin.

"Sorry, Marie, I'm tripping. It was a joke."

She put on a sad face. So did Satish. Hell.

I felt kind of bad. I had been making fun of Big Marie earlier, calling her B.M. for short. But she was a nice girl, doing it to pay for school. Studying to be a nurse. I was dealing speed to pay my tuition, so I understood.

"Tell you what, Marie—why don't I just come in and play some songs while you work?"

26

Her eyes brightened.

"Really? You mean it?"

"Sure."

We went in. There was a broken down recliner in one corner by the window, and a mattress in the middle of the floor. I took the chair.

Marie went over to the mattress and dropped the towel. Then she laid herself out and in a stunning phone-sex voice purred: "I'm *ready*."

The door opened and Seth came in. He was out of it, far past the point that I'd even know where my dick was, let alone get it hard. He was followed, timidly, by Satish.

"Thought I'd take yer place at the card table," Seth slurred. Marie rolled her eyes and looked at me.

"He's all right," I said.

Marie got on all fours. Satish went around to her front and fumbled with his zipper.

"So this your first time, hon?" Marie asked sweetly. Satish nodded. I kept playing. I started working my way through "The Harder They Come," and when I got to the payoff, I put my all into it, moaning and wailing for all it was worth: "OOO-ooo, the harder they CO-O-OME..."

In my peripheral vision I could see the three bodies moving in time to the music. It was too much. I turned completely around in the chair and stared out the window.

There was an audience. Four or five guys were crouched down, trying to look through the tattered curtain. I made eye contact with one and he whispered to me.

"Hey, open the curtain a little more so we can see!"

"Beer and pot," I said. "Bring some and I'll do it."

There was a burst of harsh whispers—"go on!" "get it!" "hurry up!"—and he scurried off. I went back to my singing:

This is the day
of the expanding man...

The frat brother came back with the beer and pot, and I opened the curtain so they could see.

"All right, man!"

"Yeah! Thanks a lot!"

They call Alabama
the Crimson Tide—

I sang for about an hour while Marie serviced another dozen or so. When it was over she thanked me, and we talked for a while.

"I do a lot of work around campus," she said, "I'd love to have someone like you working with me. I could pay you pretty well."

I told her that it was certainly a unique offer, and if I was ever back in the area I'd look her up.

There haven't been many times in my life when I've done a job for no pay and enjoyed it, let alone been offered a career opportunity that actually sounded attractive. Marie offered me both. I hope she got herself through school okay. And I bet, if she did, that she's one hell of a nurse right now.

Happy Finish

Missy was a virgin and she wanted to get laid. But she had a problem: none of the boys she liked were interested, and she wouldn't put out for the ones who were. She talked about it a lot, but I didn't mind. The more she complained the harder she worked my back.

"I'm so horny all the time," she'd groan. Then she'd lean into a big knot beneath my shoulder blade and something would pop.

"Guhhhhh," I'd reply.

I don't remember exactly how it started, but I think we were both a bit drunk after a party and the subject of massages had come up. Missy lived down the hall from me in the dorm. I had never given a massage before, so Missy showed me what to do. "You just imagine what would feel good to you," she said, "then do that to the other person." It sounded simple enough. I tried it. It worked. After a while I got pretty good. Missy would smile, and sometimes she'd sigh, give a little gasp or a pleased giggle as I worked on her. Mostly she'd just moan softly.

Missy was a real farm girl, from somewhere down in southern Illinois. That's why she was so strong, she said, and why her hands were like a man's. She said she had learned by giving her father massages every night when he came in from the fields, ever since she was a little girl. She had big, strong hands. They were the most beautiful hands I'd ever seen, and I told her so.

At the time I was fucking some bubbly little slut from Connecticut. She had walked into my room the first night of the semester, closed the door and dropped her robe. I was spoiled. Sex was easy, sex was obvious. Missy and I would talk about our experiences during our sessions. I'd tell her about my sex life with the girl from Connecticut, and the obscene things we did, and how I suspected she was fucking half the dorm (I was wrong: she was actually fucking half the University). Missy had less experience but was eager to talk about it.

"There's a boy from Burton-Judson that I've gone out with a few times. Last week I gave him a blowjob in the study room."

"The one right across the hall?"

"Yes. He wanted to come here, to my room, but I wouldn't let him. I don't really like him, but I like giving blowjobs. I actually like the taste of a man's come."

"How about having your pussy licked? You like that too?"

"Oh yes."

"Ow."

"I'm sorry, am I being too hard?"

"No, I am. Just shift your weight a little."

Our massages became more erotic. I would gently stroke Missy's ankles with my fingertips, and watch with pleasure as she shuddered all over. I would gently reach between her thighs, and stroke the downy underbrush where her pubic hair began, or reach around her back and caress the sides of her breasts that were bulging against the mattress. Missy would return the favor, raking her fingernails over my ass and sometimes sucking my fingers one by one. By the end of our sessions the air would be heavy with the smell of sex. Missy's inner thighs would be damp and sticky, like the front of my underwear. I would leave Missy's room in a daze and head straight to my Connecticut slut's room. If she was out screwing somebody else I'd go back to my room and smell my fingers as I jerked off. And on those increasingly rare occasions when I did find my little New England girlfriend at home, I would think of Missy during sex. No matter how close we came, Missy and I never crossed the line, never so much as kissed. It was Tantric massage, an agonizing bit of foreplay where the tension became more exciting than any imaginable release. Sometimes the best sex is the sex you never have.

My friends all assumed I was fucking Missy; even my slutty girlfriend thought so. I'd just nod and smile my coolest smile and say, "We're friends, nothing more."

I once heard it said that there are two reasons for doing anything: the good reason, and the real reason. I told myself, with a callow chuckle, that to get involved with Missy would be to lose the beautiful sexual tension in her virginal hands. Once we were sleeping together, I reasoned, we would lose the intense erotic charge between us, like static on a doorknob. She would want to cuddle, and hold hands, and talk silly talk. I convinced myself that by not having sex we were giving each other something much better. That was the good reason. The real reason was that I could fuck a slut from Connecticut until the slutty cows came home, but sleeping with Missy would mean something—it would have meant a relationship, and a relationship meant being honest and close and sharing yourself with someone. What could I tell her? I had no home. Home was a place you felt safe, where

31

you were welcome, where the people looked out for each other and helped each other. How could I bring a girl home to that apartment on Long Island overlooking the oil tanks and the shopping mall, that depressing place with the dingy furniture and all the cats and their smell everywhere? Home was a phone call I got every month telling me to send another check, another chunk of the college money I had earned and saved, back to a woman who said she needed it more than I did. Home was a screw-cap bottle of rosé wine by the couch. Home was rage. I couldn't get into it with anybody, not even Missy. Especially not Missy.

Missy's room was a refuge for me, a cozy place she had all to herself, and which she had decorated as if she had always lived there. There was warm soothing light, big soft pillows, pretty curtains. It didn't look like a dorm room, and when I went in there I felt safe and secure. And I was terrified of losing that.

In the spring of freshman year I got a bad case of mono. I lost 30 pounds and spit up green mucus and blood for six weeks. I had to take a leave that semester and head home, I was so sick. My last night at school Missy threw a party for me in her room. I was delirious and on heavy pain medication but I remember a bunch of us sitting around, watching her nice color television. I lay on the bed with Missy and I remember as the people drifted out of her room I finally dozed off and she put her arms around me and held me like that all night. I might have been delirious but just before I passed out I thought I heard her crying softly.

My first week back sophomore year I ran into Missy at a party. She had the same ripped faded jeans on, but her hair was done a little differently. We wound up back in my room and celebrated our reunion with a couple of quick massages. When she had finished I lay contentedly on my stomach and she sat at the edge of the bed. I had worked at a nature preserve over the summer, and while I was there I had met a beautiful laughing girl with a Toyota hatchback, who showed me how to drive a stick shift and taught me much else besides. I told Missy about the job, but not the rest. I asked Missy how her summer was, and her shoulders slumped.

"I'm still a virgin," she sighed.

"Let's go back to the party," I said.

I still think about Missy a lot. Sometimes late at night I light a few candles and lie in bed and imagine she's there. I can feel her strong, confident fingers touching and stroking me, kneading out the tension in my neck and shoulders, telling me everything will be all right. Only in my fantasies we don't stop with a massage, and at some point I turn over and pull her down and she gives herself to me. We make love, again and again, with no chance of heartbreak, fear or regret. And for the thousandth time I come across my belly and dream myself to sleep.

NoLa Tango

I was walking in a bad part of town, about an hour before dawn. I saw a shadow moving across the street, towards me.

"Mithter..."

There was nothing around us but empty lots and bombed-out buildings. The shadow passed through the pool of light cast by a single bare bulb hanging over the intersection. He was short and stocky, coming on like some crazy bouncing meatball.

"Hey mithter...MITHTER!"

I gripped the knife in my pocket. I squared off and faced him.

"What the hell do you want?" I growled.

"Thuck yo dick?"

"What?"

When he spoke I could see he had no front teeth.

"Yo dick. Fo thwee dollahs I thuck yo dick."

I loosened my grip on the knife.

"Shit, man, do I really look like I need to pay for it?"

The meatball smiled, a crazy toothless grin.

"No, mithter...I pay YOU."

"Not interested. Sorry."

"Fo?"

I waved my hand and kept walking. I was afraid that if he offered five, I'd say yes.

A few blocks later I found the place. *Work-Rite Employment Services.* They only paid minimum but it was cash at the end of the day, no waiting, no bullshit. The doors opened at five and the bums started shuffling in shortly after. Most of them were looking for work but a lot of them just needed to sleep. There were big signs posted: NO SLEEPING. I looked around the room: everybody was sleeping.

I went up to the window. A bored and tired looking clerk asked me to write my information on an index card. Then there was some kind of liability form, absolving Work-Rite Employment Services, Inc., of any responsibility if something happened to me. There were some yes or no questions: had I ever been convicted of a felony? Did I have any medical problems that could prevent me from doing certain kinds of work? Had I ever been treated for alcoholism? Drug addiction? Depression? I checked off 'no' down the line, and handed the papers back. The man drawled that they'd call my name if they had anything. I took my seat with the rest of the bums and waited.

I was one of the first called. It didn't surprise me. I was the youngest in the room by twenty years, and probably the only one who had taken a hot bath that week. I was also one of the only ones awake.

The first job was delivering booze. I was driven out to a warehouse and assigned to one of the drivers. It was a big truck and we had a full load. There were deliveries at liquor stores all over the city. It was easy work. It was a hot, hazy morning, and I liked sitting up high in the truck and looking down at the other cars. The driver, Patrick, had been doing the job for ten years, he was supporting a family. We'd pull up to place, Patrick would go inside with the invoice, talk with the manager or whoever was on duty, then come out and we'd put together the order. We took our time, and he asked me a lot of questions about New York, and I asked him questions about New Orleans. He was a nice guy; we got along well.

We did a few deliveries, then when we got to the next place Patrick asked me to handle it. I took the invoice inside and spoke to the owner. He asked where Patrick was, and who I was, and I told him and he was satisfied. I went back to the truck to put together the order. Patrick was already in the back of the truck. He didn't look happy.

"Come up here a minute," he said. "We got a problem."

I climbed up into the truck. "What is it?"

"We've got breakage." He pointed to a case of whiskey. "See the box?"

"Yes."

"That's the problem."

"It looks fine to me."

Patrick shook his head. He had work boots on, and he brought his right leg back and smashed it into the side of the case. There was a crack and a moment later the side of the box grew wet, and the truck filled up with the smell of whiskey. Patrick smiled.

"Like I said, we got breakage."

He pulled open the box. "It ain't too bad. Only lost one." He pulled out one of the unbroken bottles. "Can't sell 'em when they're broken," he said, unscrewing the cap. He took a swig and handed me the bottle. I hesitated.

"You sure this is okay?" I asked. Patrick laughed.

"Shit, I've been doing this for ten years. One of the perks of the job."

I wasn't going to argue. I shrugged and took a swig.

We passed the bottle back and forth a few times, then continued on the run.

The rest of the day was the same: drive to next store, make the delivery, and take a little hit off our bottle. We took our time, stopped for a long lunch, and vocally expressed our admiration to the pretty women that walked by.

After the last stop, Patrick and I shared a last drink, killed the bottle, then Patrick took a crowbar and positioned the empty bottle over the case. He swung the crowbar expertly, and the bottle broke neatly. He put the crowbar down.

"Like I said," he drawled, "we lost *two* bottles."

Patrick dropped me off at the labor pool. He signed my timesheet, and didn't deduct for our long lunch hour. He said his regular helper was coming back the next day, otherwise he'd hire me back on. I thanked him and hopped out of the truck. Then I went in, collected my pay, and the clerk asked if I would be coming back the next day. I gave a disinterested shrug and said I didn't know.

On the walk back home I felt warm inside, from the whiskey and the day. I picked up a 12-pack and some cigarettes from the corner grocery and went home to celebrate.

My room was on St. Charles, in the most run-down house on the block. The hallway smelled mildewy, the paint was peeling, and every fixture and appliance was old beyond decency. Still, by Manhattan standards, it was a palace: high ceilings, a fireplace, and an enormous claw foot tub. The rent was fifty dollars a week. The house had originally been the servants' quarters for the main house next door, which was where the landlord lived. My kitchen was built into the second floor walkway that originally connected the two houses. It was suspended between the two buildings, over an alley. I would fry an egg in the morning and look out the window down the alley and watch the trolleys as they rattled by, clanging their bells, the palm trees swaying in the muggy breeze.

Randy had told me about the labor pool. Randy was a Vietnam vet who lived in a dark place on the first floor in back. Randy was a heavy drinker, and more than a little crazy. Some nights we'd sit and drink in my room and it would begin. I'd be sitting quietly, drinking my beer and listening to the radio, and he'd start yelling.

"Coxsackie! Ha ha! If old man Peabody didn't shiv the bejesus out of that old sow, ha ha! Mercy buckets we can't be having that, now, can we? Coxsackie!"

It went on like that, sometimes for half an hour, a rambling disconnected dialog that I couldn't decipher. All I know is that Coxsackie figured prominently in all his monologues. In a rare lucid moment, Randy told me he had done time in Sing-Sing, but when I tried to get the details, his replies would get more and more incomprehensible. Just when I thought I would have to kick him out, or call the funny farm, a song might come on the radio, and he'd stop mid-sentence and say, with a completely calm voice, something like, "Is this *The Who*? Did you know that Pete Townshend used a modified Gibson SG with a coil-splitter switch for the bridge pick-up? It's true. That's how he got that out-of-phase sound on 'Baba O'Reilly'."

I went back to the labor pool, but it wasn't the same. That magical first day with Patrick was never repeated. I cleared trash, mopped spills, built sheds, loaded trucks. The pay was low and the work was hard, sometimes fiendishly so. Once I spent 18 hours with three other bums replacing an engine in a tugboat on the Mississippi. We had to lower the engine, an enormous thing, through a hole in the deck and move it into place. The total distance couldn't have been more than ten feet; we moved about six inches an hour. It was brutal, dangerous work. At the end of the day, I collected my money. There were less than fifty dollars in the envelope. I had to find a better job.

I took some days off and walked through the French Quarter. I stopped at any place that had a help wanted sign. I filled out plenty of forms, but they all wanted a phone number, and I didn't have a phone. I would tell that that I just moved into town and the phone would be installed soon, and they would give me a look and that would be that.

Finally I came upon a steak house, an old and dignified looking place. The smell of the sizzling steaks drew me closer. It was heavenly. There was a small sign in the window: *Waiter wanted.* I had always told myself I would never wait tables again. The last time I had thrown a lobster in a customer's face. But then, I hadn't been as hungry as I was now. I went in.

To my surprise, the manager offered me the job. The place was busy, he said, and he was in a bind. There were a number of conventions in town, and the place was going to be packed for the next several weeks. He told me I could start the next afternoon, for a trial run.

On my way out I looked more closely at the tables around me: they were filled with fat, grease-smeared businessmen, in town for the plumbing convention, or the widget conference. They were eating and drinking, laughing and yelling at the staff.

"Hey boy, BOY! Ovah heah, boy!"

I watched as one of them grabbed at a waitress as she tried to get by. "Mah, yer lookin' mahty purty liddle lady, whoop! Gotcha! Haw haw haw haw haw!"

I walked out the door. I didn't go back.

For a couple of weeks I tried to find something. No luck. My money was almost gone and the rent was coming due, so on the last possible day I reluctantly went back to the labor pool.

My next assignment was at a cement factory, out in Metairie. My job was shoveling the cement dust that fell off the conveyor belt back into a furnace, where it got sifted, scooped back up into the conveyor, and jiggled right back to the floor. It was a farce. For eight hours I shoveled, a dust mask suffocating me, my shirt off and the sweat pouring down, my pants literally soaked all the way through. It was Indian summer and the outside temperature was in the nineties, on top of the inferno in front of me, inside of me.

At the end of the day the foreman drove me back to the main road, to a bus stop. Apparently the company was too far outside the city for them to drive me back to the labor pool. I couldn't wait to get on a cool, air-conditioned bus and go to sleep.

I studied the map. I would take the bus to the end of the line, and then switch to the streetcar that would take me home. Using my thumb as a measure, I figured it was about a six-mile ride to the streetcar, and then another five or six miles to my house.

The bus came, and I got on. I sat in the seat nearest the driver and started counting my change. I had just enough for the fare. I told the driver I needed a transfer.

"Where you going?" he asked. I told him. He shook his head.

"Transfers ain't no good on the streetcar. We're in a different parish out here, the lines are independent. You'll have to pay again when you get to the streetcar line."

I had enough change for the bus or the streetcar, but not both. My body was already stiffening; I was afraid that by the time I had to get off the bus I wouldn't be able to walk. I figured it would be better to walk the first leg of the trip home, then get on the streetcar for the last part. I asked the driver to let me off at the next stop, and he obliged.

I started the long trek home. The sun was beginning to sink, and I suddenly felt very cold. My pants, which had been soaked in sweat and cement dust all day, began to dry, and as they dried they hardened. They felt twice as heavy as they did before. I was wearing concrete pants! They fought me every step of the way: the knees crackled as I walked; my skinny abdomen knocked like a bell in the loose and hardened waistline of my jeans. It was my Waterloo, my Alamo, my death march. And at the end of the misery, there were twenty-five dollars with my name on them.

The walk took three hours. It wasn't a walk, really, more of a shuffle. I had to hold up my pants to keep the weight from dragging them around my ankles. It was now night, and I passed bar after bar, feeling the cement dust in my nostrils, my sinuses, the back of my throat. There were pickup trucks parked out front, country music blaring and the warm comforting neon. I couldn't afford so much as a glass of beer. I finally stopped at another bus stop to see how much farther I had to go. I got my bearings and realized that the streetcar stop was only a few blocks away! I was saved!

41

I began to walk again when a compact car pulled up alongside me. A little guy leaned over and rolled down the passenger window.

"Hey," he called to me. "You look like you're dragging. Need a lift somewhere?"

"Thanks," I said, "but my streetcar stop is just up ahead."

"Where's your final destination?"

"Near Lee Circle," I told him.

"That's not far from where I'm going. Hop in, I'll drive you."

I got in the car. I had my knife, as always, so I didn't feel too threatened. Even if he pulled a gun, I'd have a chance. Then I saw a flash of something metallic between his legs. I was about to jump out of the car when I saw it was a can of Bud Light.

"Want a beer?" he asked. "I got some in the back."

"Sure, thanks," I said. I pulled one off and opened it.

"My name's Van," he said, extending a hand.

"John," I said, shaking it, "John Mellor. Nice to meet you."

"Likewise," he smiled. He began to drive, and we sat in silence, drinking our beers. Then Van spoke again. "I don't mean to be rude, John, but I was wondering: would you like to go get a drink somewhere? I know a number of nice cocktail lounges nearby." I was going to say no, but changed my mind. What the hell, I thought, it was one of the better offers I'd gotten recently.

"Sure, let's go," I said. "But I have to warn you, I haven't got a cent on me."

"I know," Van said, "I figured that's why you were walking."

We ended up in the Circleview Tavern, one of the dark and dirty dives near the labor pool. Stench, filth, and a maudlin jukebox. Tall cans of *Old Milwaukee* for eighty-five cents. I drank five or six, quickly, and Van had the bartender set us up some

some shots. He asked me about my astrological sign, what kind of dreams I had, my sexual habits, my relationship with my parents. He told me he was sad and lonely and had a big house in the country and would take good care of me. I told him my fiancée was waiting for me at home, and that she was three months pregnant and needed me around. Van asked me to come home with him; I told him another time, maybe. He asked me to go to another bar, some place quiet where we could be alone.

He put up a protest when I said I had to go, but when he realized it was hopeless Van asked me if he could kiss me on the cheek. What the hell, I thought, and he did and then I left. I waited until I was on the sidewalk and then I wiped my cheek.

I continued working for the cement company. They took me off the shoveling work and gave me easier things to do. I always made sure to bring enough money to get home at night. After a couple of weeks, I asked the foreman why he didn't just hire me on, so he wouldn't have to go through the agency. The foreman said sure, he could do that, because I was a good worker and dependable. He would even give me a raise.

The next morning one of the foreman's boys, a big guy named Jeff, picked me up at the labor pool and started driving me to work. I noticed we were going a different way, and I asked him what was up.

"We've got a big new job outside town," he explained. "It's a good job, construction and other stuff. You'll see. You can learn a lot with us, we're a good company and you're a smart guy. I hear we're going to be hiring you. The boss says you're doing a mighty fine job. Believe me, if the boss likes what you're doing, he'll take good care of you."

I didn't say anything, but I was beaming inside. Jeff pulled the truck into a convenience store parking lot.

"Hell, I know this sounds crazy, but what do you say we celebrate?"

"At a convenience store?"

"Go on in and get us a couple of beers."

"Really?" I looked at the clock on the dashboard. It wasn't even seven a.m.

"Hell, it's a long drive, at least another hour. Might as well pass the time."

"Okay. What do you want?"

"Whatever. Don't matter. Just make sure you get a receipt."

Jeff gave me a five and I went in and got two tall beers, paid for them, asked for a receipt, and went back to the truck. I gave him the change and receipt and opened a beer and handed it to him. He waved it away.

"No thanks, not just yet. You go ahead."

I drank the first beer. So this is what they meant by the Big Easy! Sometimes there really was God all of a sudden. When I finished it I offered Jeff the other, but again he begged off, saying he wasn't feeling right just then but by all means, I should have it.

I had it.

All that day I worked better than ever. Beer for breakfast, a sweet buzz at daybreak, and I motored through the work like it was a hot and dusty lover. The foreman and me cracked jokes, I led the others in song, we took plenty of cigarette breaks and talked about the differences between North and South, black and white, blondes and brunettes.

The next day was Friday, my last day working through the labor pool. On Monday I would be working for the construction company directly.

I got to the labor pool on time. I went up to the window, filled my card. The guy behind the bulletproof glass gave me a look and I took my seat. As usual, the waiting room was filled with the wreckage of humanity: tattered men muttered to invisible companions, fished their orifices for edibles, snored and groaned and belched and spat. It was an abomination. I was relieved to be leaving it all behind, to be embarking on my new career. I looked at the time. Somebody should have shown up by now. Ten minutes went by, then twenty. I went back to the window.

"Any word from my company?" I asked. The clerk asked me which company. I told him. He shuffled some papers, not looking at me.

"They were here already and left," he said.

"Are you sure? There must be some kind of mistake!"

"I'm sure. And no, it's no mistake." Then he looked at me and said: "I don't think I have anything for you today."

I was halfway home before I got it. The receipt. Of course. He had tricked me, the bastard! I hadn't wanted those beers, it hadn't been my idea, I never would have drunk them if he hadn't offered, if I hadn't thought I'd have been rude saying no.

That night I lay in bed, drinking beer and thinking about steak. There was a knock on the door. I asked who it was. Randy, the voice answered. Go away, I said. He did.

The Boy In The Bed

I don't know why I even answered the ad. I'd been out of work before, but maybe I was feeling more desperate than usual, I don't remember. Before I knew it I was sitting in the dark and overstuffed foyer of a Park Avenue apartment, giving my name and business to a nervous German cook

The position was for a companion, for a sick young man. Duties included shopping, errands, and conversation. I had this vague notion I'd be paid to talk, maybe play video games. I had no experience in home care but was hoping my conversational skills would get me by. The only things I wouldn't do were wiping somebody's ass or cleaning a bedpan. I had to remember to mention that.

The cook went down the hallway to announce my arrival. A minute later she returned, making calisthenic gestures with her fists. "The lady will see you now," she intoned curtly, then was gone.

46

When I reached the end of the corridor I looked left. A ghostly noise was emanating from the dark bedroom at the end of the side hallway, the familiar whirrs and clicks of a breathing apparatus. I could see the outline of a hospital bed, and what looked like an IV drip; against one wall some kind of monitoring device emitted little green pulses and blips on a screen. To my right was another bedroom. I went right.

Mrs. Brace received me from bed. She was a large woman, huge. Her slightest move sent shockwaves across the sagging mattress that engulfed her. The precious few inches still free from her sprawl were occupied by an array of equipment: boxes of tissues, remote controls, intercom, a bell, two telephones, and a bulging address book. I took particular notice of the address book, as I had a feeling I was going to become intimately acquainted with many of its listings.

She cleared her throat, sending a ripple down her chins and causing the box springs to groan in complaint. Her eyes narrowed to beams.

"So, Mr. Hall, why do you want this job?"

"The ad said flexible hours, and the money is right."

"Yes. The money, I see. Do you have any experience with illness?"

"No ma'am."

"Are you some kind of actor or musician?"

"I play guitar in a band."

"I see. My Francis is a musician too. Or rather, he was. He's generally too weak to play any more, but he does love his music. Eddie—that's Mister Brace—sometimes takes Francis to a concert, which is of course a huge to-do, with the special van and equipment. We try to indulge him as much as possible now, because we don't know how long he'll be able to do even that much."

Her voice trailed off.

"Can I ask what's wrong with Francis?"

"Of course. If I am to expect your honesty you must expect mine. Francis has MS, which, as you may or may not know, is incurable."

"Yes ma'am. May I ask how old he is?"

"Twenty-six."

"I'm very sorry."

"Thank you. We do the best we can. We want to make things as comfortable for him as possible with whatever time he has left."

"Of course."

On the far wall I spied a picture. I realized with a shock that it was of a young Mrs. Brace. She was sprawled across a leopard-spotted chaise in a tight, slinky evening gown. It was a black and white photo, with the signature of the photographer scrawled along a lower corner. I guessed early 1960s. Mrs. Brace was shapely and buxom, still thirty years and a few billion calories from the figure she cut now, wheezing and groaning and committing unspeakable offenses against a box spring.

Mrs. Brace caught me staring at the photo.

"Oh that," she sighed. "I was a pretty young thing, wasn't I?"

"Yes ma'am."

"I had a night club act, I was a *chanteuse.*" She sighed. "Those were my salad days."

You should have skipped the dressing, I thought.

"It's very flattering." I said.

Mrs. Brace had been wearing a dreamy sort of expression, which disappeared and was replaced with a scowl.

"But we're not hear to talk about me. Are you quick on your feet, Mr. Hall?"

"I think so."

"Good, because there's nothing I hate more than a laggard. The last boy we had in here took dreadful advantage. He took absolutely forever to do the simplest things. Then I found out he was passing the time at the nearest bar."

There goes that idea, I thought.

"I will not tolerate such abuse, do you understand?"

"Yes ma'am."

"Good. What are you doing now?"

I checked to see if I was pulling at my crotch again. I wasn't.

"I mean, are you free for a few hours, as a sort of trial? We're a little short-handed at the moment."

Mrs. Brace saw my hesitation. Her face darkened.

"Don't worry, you'll be paid."

I wasn't worried about the money. The whole thing depressed me. I wanted to run out of there and never come back.

"Sure," I said weakly, "I'm available."

"Fine. I need you to run to the market. There's a Gristede's on Third Avenue. Hilda will give you the list, and here are some things to add to it." She waved a slip of paper in my direction, a little white flag flapping in her fat fingers. I took it and we stared at each other.

"Yes?"

"How am I supposed to pay for this?"

Mrs. Brace groaned again. She was a hard woman but her hardness seemed pleading at the same time. But pleading for what or for whom I couldn't say.

"We've got an account. Hilda will give you the details."

I went into the kitchen and talked with Hilda, the nervous, sliced-up neurotic German cook who'd shown me in. Hilda wrung her hands constantly and dispatched me with the cold ruthless efficiency her kind are so properly known for.

As I exited the plush lobby into the stultifying air of the July afternoon, the withering heat reflecting off the asphalt felt like a cool wave on a tropical beach; the horns blaring on Park Avenue, the dowagers scraping dog shit from the sidewalk, filled me with happiness and lighthearted joy. I walked in no great hurry in the direction of Gristede's. Mrs. Brace was a tough customer but she wasn't going to get me jumping through any hoops. I knew that however fast I came back she'd roll her eyes and cluck her tongue and mumble about how she'd nearly starved. I was twenty years old and had already had two dozen jobs.

I kept thinking about the photo on the bedroom wall. I could see the future Mrs. Brace taking the stage, against a deep red velvet curtain and in a smoky spotlight. Her hungry cat eyes scan the smoky tables of inebriated commuters with a fragile strength, trying to keep the old devil magic working.

The band begins the number: maracas and a castanet, brushes on a snare. A weary divorcee in a frayed tuxedo plucks off a descending riff on the double bass as the clarinetist tosses off a facsimile of a Middle Eastern scale and she draws a hefty flank up exposing a ripe knee. She peers smoothly into the crowd sizing up man after man, the same way every night, and expertly checks them off her list: too drunk, too old, too married. She's already had enough of their rough pornography, their adulterous gropes and fanny-slapping promises about a good ride and a real man being all she needs. No. She's had enough of that.

The she sees him, drinking a Stinger, entranced by the show. He's the only one sitting alone, which touches her as a kind of inner strength. She can tell through the smoky haze of the room, with the cheap colored lights flaring in her eyes, that he's dressed well, wearing a superb gold watch and exquisite cuff links. He looks all right, he's not a regular.

She arranges a meeting, makes it look accidental. Jackpot: he is a successful businessman and even more successful heir, simple and naive from Protestant money-love. She appears bored, condescends to let him buy her a drink, occasionally leaves his table to converse with the loud, cigar-smoking men she normally wouldn't acknowledge. She keeps Mr. Brace waiting until the end of the night, and when he gratefully asks her for a dinner engagement she acquiesces. From that night on he is a small, mineral-rich moon circling the vast fluid expanse of his beloved.

They fall in love. Park Avenue, glittering parties, Lincoln Center. There's talk of polishing the act, bringing it to Broadway, using influence to get her an interview with a leading producer. But she wants out, she's tired of the clubs, the leering men and other vagaries of performing life. She wants to be his wife, the mother of his children, and he wants to protect and provide. They want only to fulfill their dreams and desires together. So many tragedies start the same way. Why?

As I made my way down the supermarket aisles I watched the nannies and young mothers pushing their kids in carts, trying to make sense of life by comparing the price of chicken breasts. I imagined going to bed with all of them. If I were John Cheever, I thought, I'd strike up a conversation, take one of them home, and that would be that.

But I wasn't, and besides I didn't have the time. I had to get back to the apartment. Francis needed me.

51

Meticulous Movers

I was the smallest so I rode hump. Jack, the pudgy blonde foreman and driver, would reach between my legs, massage the black knob and start the Mae West routine.

"Oooh, is that a stick shift or are you just glad to see me?"

The other guys loved this, they'd laugh and hiss and we'd rattle down the street. It was better when we pulled up to a stop light, it would distract attention from me.

"Hey sailor, nice ass!" Bongo would yell. "¡Que rico!" Hector would sing-song. It was an education, and perversely satisfying, to watch some cocky and confident-looking straights—frat boys, b-boys, yuppies and guidos—look confused, then enraged, then embarrassed and finally defeated as a bunch of muscle-bound queens made lewd sexual comments about their anatomy, kissing and sucking and slapping the outside of the truck. I don't remember if I ever joined in their wolf whistling. I probably wouldn't tell you anyway.

Meticulous Movers was owned by a guy named Barry. Barry looked like he'd always play the part of a shady, unsympathetic minor figure in the B-movie of life. He was little, mustached, with greasy matted hair and pockmarked skin. The sort of guy who ate hard-boiled eggs every day for lunch.

The company was operating on the fringe—trucks weren't up to code, tires were bald, equipment was shoddy—but the work was there and the pay was good. This was the late 80s, New York City, and we were a gay moving company. There was plenty of work. We all just wished there wasn't. I'd see the photos on a dresser or nightstand, the happy couple at Fire Island or Key West, and now the boxed clothes, the personal effects going to thrift shops, antique stores, being returned to family or close friends. And the surviving partner moving to a smaller place or back to Minnesota, or in with a new lover. I saw their haggard faces, tired, resilient, sometimes looking decades older than they had in photos from only a few years earlier. The guys I worked with always seemed to know what to say to put them at ease, make them laugh, and the customers were almost entirely grateful and generous. I kept my mouth shut and did what I was told.

The job carried with it its share of good feeling; we knew we were helping people, but work is work, which is to say almost uniformly pointless and sprit crushing, and Meticulous Movers was no exception. It was backbreaking work, and my tolerance for some of the pissy bullshit the guys dished out grew ever thinner. Jack always treated me decently but the others would go into their A-list routine, the wicked stepsister act. Come here, hurry up, do this, do that: it was like being trapped with three Joan Crawfords on Oscar night. In fact I believe Hector actually did have his own Joan Crawford act, down at some bar on Grove Street.

"C'mon breeder boy, what are you waiting for?"

"Get your mind off pussy, dear, and pick up that box!"

"Be careful, ninny, that vase is Ming!"

Usually it didn't bother me, I could understand or at least rationalize it. Then I'd think, shit, I've never persecuted gays, why should I be understanding? More than once I was close to dropping the business end of a Louis Whatever armoire, in the middle of some impossibly twisting upper west side brownstone staircase.

"Lift up your end, little man!"

"Fuck you!" I'd scream, enraged and out of breath, and the hissing would begin again.

One Friday night, after a particularly brutal week, we were driving back to the office. Everybody was quiet for a change. After we parked Jack told us that the company was going under, and that if we had been thinking of getting new jobs it was a good time to start looking.

Monday morning I called in sick, took the PATH train to 9th Street, and walked to Washington Square to sit and read the classifieds. I was still harboring vague aspirations of being a musician, so after checking under "mail clerk" and "messenger"— and carefully avoiding "moving company"—I saw something under "music":

Music Co. Seeks Self-Starter
Renowned commercial music house needs messenger. Your
interests will shape your growth. Call Alan at...

I finished my bagel and coffee, found some change in my pocket, and went to a pay phone. "Wow," the person named Alan said, "that was fast. You're the first to call. Are you able to come in today?"

No, I told him, I was terribly busy, but tomorrow would be fine. I wasn't trying to be coy, I just realized that I had no resume, suit, dress shoes, or even a clean shirt. I took care of basic wardrobe needs at a Hoboken thrift shop, and that night sat down at my trusty battleship gray Royal manual and banged out something that sounded reasonable. The next morning I called in sick to Meticulous Movers again and got ready for the interview.

I was hired on the spot. Judging from the way Alan looked at me I think my tenure with Meticulous Movers, however brief, helped immensely. When the paperwork was done I celebrated by walking to 57th street and seeing a Milton Avery exhibit. I had strange ways of celebrating back then.

When I got home to Hoboken that afternoon my girlfriend was lying on the bed. She was independently wealthy. We had been living together for about three weeks.

"I got the job!" I told her.

"That's nice," she said. She was looking at her stomach.

"What's wrong?"

She kept looking at her stomach. Then she began to cry.

A few weeks later I was taking the uptown E train, on a run. I heard a plaintive voice calling out from the end of the car:

"Good morning ladies and gentlemen, I'm homeless, and I'm selling this paper to try to raise money for food...." The voice sounded familiar, but I couldn't see him through the crowd.

"...Just a few weeks ago I was the owner of a moving company, and then I went out of business. I lost everything. I'm selling these papers to get some money so I can find a place to live and get back on my feet...." I looked up and saw Barry coming down the aisle, selling newspapers for his egg money. I don't know if he saw me or not, but as he passed he seemed to avoid looking in my direction, even walking past someone to my right who was holding out some change. I won't say I was glad, because I wasn't, but I couldn't help but remember how I had to threaten him to get my last paycheck, and how Jack had stepped between us and let his hand linger on my chest just a second too long.

That night after work I was sitting in my favorite bar, drinking a Cajun martini and listening to Esquerita on the jukebox. Bill the bartender came over.

"The next one's on that gentleman over there." I turned on the stool and looked to a table in the corner and there was Jack, sitting with a good-looking man. He smiled warmly at me. There were some problems he wouldn't know, and I was glad for that. We raised our glasses, and I mouthed my thank you.

Club It Up

1.

I got off the five-nineteen express and went across the street to Dingle's. Dingle's is one of those ten cent Buffalo wings, ladies drink Jell-O shots free all night suburban bars that advertised on local radio, with a gravel-voiced announcer shouting over the sound of a car engine revving. Classic rock cover bands, Monday night football on a projection screen. If I stayed on Long Island much longer I would kill myself. I knew several people who already had.

The bartender had just pushed an overpriced pint in front of me when someone slapped me on the back. I turned around. It was Ted Donner.

"Tim! Long time no see! I didn't know you were in town."

"I'm not. I'm just here a few more days. Then I'm moving to San Francisco."

"What's out there for you?"

"Nothing."

"What are you going to do?"

"I don't know."

Ted laughed. "You haven't changed. How's the music business treating you?"

"I'm retired."

"I thought you were working for a big jingle house."

"I quit."

"Are you kidding? People would kill for that job!" "Don't you think they knew that?"

"I heard you wrote a song for some big movie."

"I did. I got screwed on that too."

"Bummer. Can I join you?"

"Please."

Ted sat down and ordered two beers. I had always liked Ted. I had known him since grade school. In high school we each had our own bands and used to jam with each other at parties and dances, and bring our acoustic guitars to late-night golf course grope fests. But Ted had always been serious about making it in music. Whenever his band played he would build a whole two-level stage out of plywood and milk crates, and rig a light show that he would control with his feet during the show. Ted had always been a hard rock guy: Outlaws, Zeppelin, Molly Hatchet. He still had the long, curly locks down past his shoulders, and wore cowboy boots and silk shirts.

I had never been very focused. I just sort of dicked around, doing one thing for a while then moving on to something else. Bands, jingles, soundtracks, whatever. No dedication. That's what my last girlfriend had said, that I just couldn't seem to finish anything I started. Right. I finished the beer and ordered two more.

"You should see the place I'm at now. It's a new record company out in Huntington. Lots of money behind it, great place. I'm the studio manager."

"Sounds nice."

"Want a job?"

"Are you serious?"

"Sure, we're getting really busy and I'm short handed right now."

"What would I have to do?"

"Not much at first. We have to finish the construction first. But eventually you'd be writing songs."

"Let's have another," I said.

Ted told me about the place. It was called Monsieur Records, he said they wanted to be the next Motown. Monsieur had been founded a few years earlier by a millionaire named Izzy Klein, who Ted claimed was some kind of financial genius. They had started out doing rock, then jazz, and now they were focusing on pop and dance music. They wanted to hire songwriters to build a catalog of original material, which the company could then release. They wanted to develop their own sound, their own artists, everything.

Ted made everything sound magical, happening, exciting. I told myself I wasn't really interested. The whole point for me was to get the hell *off* of Long Island. But the more Ted talked the better it sounded. He kept saying, "Just give it a shot, come out and see the place." I agreed, and we had a round of Jell-O shots to celebrate.

The next day Ted drove me out to the studio. It was in an industrial park in Huntington, near the Railroad station. We pulled up to an unassuming brick building with a small sign over the door: Monsieur Records.

We went inside. Ted hadn't exaggerated, the place was really nice. There was more construction to be done but there was already a lot of impressive equipment. They were sparing no expense to make the place first-class.

I spent the day hanging around, watching and talking, and before I knew it I was doing stuff. I helped set something up, fixed a computer glitch, carried a box down the hall. I went back the next day, and the day after that. Ted offered to pay me for my time, and I made it clear it was only temporary, that any day I was going to book my flight to California.

At the end of the week Ted handed me a paycheck, then took me to a strip club near the studio. A glassy-eyed dancer with bruises on her legs and a caesarean scar gyrated to ZZ Top in nothing but a pair of beige pumps. I'm not usually into shoes but something about those pumps really set me off, they were the most obscene things I had ever seen. Perverted. My last girlfriend had called me that, too. Maybe if she had had a pair of beige pumps I wouldn't have dumped her.

A pile of singles appeared before me. Ted balanced one of the bills on his nose.

"Like this, dude. Watch how she does it. No hands."

"Sweet Jesus."

One week turned to two, then three. Just one more week, I'd think. San Francisco would always be there, unless it fell into the ocean, and in that case what would it matter? Monsieur wasn't a bad place to be at all. Huntington was a nice town, green and peaceful, and the studios were always quiet and dark and air-conditioned. I would go in when I had a hangover and find a dark corner and nap for an hour or two and nobody would bother me.

After about a month Ted took me into his office and showed me a stack of papers on his desk. It was a big pile, at least a foot high.

"See these? These are letters, from people who have applied for your position. There are tons of qualified people dying to work here. I'm not trying to pressure you but I know you're still talking about moving to California. If you want the job permanently you should make a decision fairly soon."

I looked down at all those applications, hundreds of them, from people desperate to break into the music business. I had seen similar piles back at the jingle house. Julliard graduates begging for a chance to clean the toilets for free, just to get a foot in the door, so they could some day make big bucks writing music for potato chips and incontinence briefs. Everywhere, it seemed, people were begging for the kinds of jobs that I just fell into. I thought of all those better qualified, dedicated and hardworking souls. Fuck it. If they spent less time dicking with their clarinets and more time drinking in bars, maybe they would get better jobs.

"I'll take it," I said.

2.

With the money I had saved I bought an old Toyota truck to get myself around. Then I found a room in a rundown old house on a dead end street, not far from the studio. My plan was to drive as little as possible. I had heard a saying that you shouldn't drink and drive because you might spill your drink. Back then I didn't know it was a joke. I'd walk.

Ted and I went back to the strip club a few more times, but that scene got old quickly, as well as expensive. I drove around after work, looking for a regular bar. It wasn't easy. Most of the places were sports bars, chain restaurants, or just noisy, overcrowded places filled with drunken college kids. I finally found my place, a dim little brick box not far from my room called The Rusty Nail. The name fit perfectly: it looked like the type of place that could give a guy tetanus just by walking into it.

There was a cast of characters who hung out at the Nail. My favorite was Ben, a 50-year old geek who wore thick glasses, read science fiction novels, and still lived at home with his mother. Another regular was Jerry, a sort of genteel ex-hippie type, who brought his guitar to the bar and would sing songs until late. He had a good voice and once in a while he would hand me the guitar and I'd do a few numbers. Then I noticed Jerry got free drinks for as long as he played, and I began bringing my guitar too. We did a lot of Neil Young, Rolling Stones, and Gram Parsons. Occasionally I'd bust out an old soul song, some Don Covay or James Carr number that would blow everybody's mind, and Jerry would pull out a harp and blow along with me.

I became a regular. Anna was the Irish bartender who ran the place. Anna liked to play Yahtzee, and wouldn't take no for an answer. I had never played before, but eventually I got into it too. The radio was always tuned to a rock station out of Connecticut, which for some reason gave the place a kind of worldly feel to me. I would leave the bar late and stumble back up route 110, past the cemetery where some of my ancestors were buried; past the mini-mall where I bought my 40-ounce beers; and then past the seedy old black man bar that I was too scared to go into. There was always some crazy scene going on in there—pimps screaming at their whores, whores screaming at their pimps, somebody running out chasing or being chased by a swinging handbag. I once saw a woman take off her shoe and hurl it at the back of some guy's head, and he spilled across the sidewalk. I always crossed the street until I was far enough past the place to cross back over and get to my room.

In the morning I'd roll out of bed, wash myself in the bathroom across the hall and get into some clothes. Then it was just a matter of walking a little further down route 110, crossing the train station parking lot and walking the last few blocks through the poor section of town to the industrial park. I'd usually get to the studio around ten, and more often than not the first thing I'd do would be to lie in one of the dark and windowless rooms and sleep for another hour.

When the construction was done Ted assigned me to one of the new composing rooms. There was track lighting with dimmer knobs, a leather sectional in one corner, and plush red carpeting. It had all the latest keyboards, samplers, and computer gear. There was even a turntable, so I could play my old albums. I was now officially a composer. My first day I went into the room, closed the door, put on a Don Covay record, dimmed the lights, and went to sleep.

Ted woke me up. "Dude!"

"Is it time to go to the strip club?"

"Ha ha! No. Okay, I got something for you to do. How'd you like to start writing some songs?"

"Sure, anything!"

"Great. Here's what I need you to do. Come up with ten song titles and give them to me at the end of the day."

"Just the titles?"

"I'll explain later." Ted left.

Strange, I thought. Maybe it was a test, or some kind of psychological screening. I got a pad and pen and made up some song titles. At the end of the day I handed him the sheet of paper and left for the night.

The next morning I was preparing for my nap when Ted came bursting in. And I mean, bursting. He was always throwing open doors, running, yelling, announcing his presence in the most obvious ways. It was annoying. He sat down and handed me something. It was my list of song titles.

"I need you to work on these," he said.

"You don't like them? You want better titles?"

"No, no," he said, "the titles are fine. What I mean is, I need you to start working on the songs themselves, the music that goes with them."

"I'm confused."

"Don't worry about it, just come up with some music for these songs. Can you do that for me?"

"Sure, but—"

"Thanks, man. You rock. That's why I hired you, because I knew I could count on you. There's just one thing. What do you want to call this project?"

"I don't understand—"

"You will, you will. Just give me a project name!"

"Ummm, how about Big-Eyed Beans From Venus?"

"Fine, fine!" Ted scribbled on the clipboard.

"Wait! I'm joking!"

"Don't worry about it, it's perfect." Ted wrote some more on the pad. "You are now producing the Big-Eyed Beans From Venus project."

I tried to protest but Ted was already gone. I consulted my list of song titles. It was all so strange, I didn't understand what the point was. More importantly, how was I going to come up with lyrics for a song called "Beige Pumps"?

I don't remember how I managed it, exactly, but I got the songs done. I threw together ten tracks, transferred them to tape, then we hired a couple of singers to lay down some vocals. When they were all done I made a cassette for Ted to listen to. The songs were terrible, but Ted was pleased.

"Thanks, Tim, you rock. I knew I could count on you."

"Ted, I don't want you to think I'm ungrateful, because I'm not, but this all seems a bit strange to me. I mean, first you ask me for titles, then a band name, and then the songs. Aren't we doing things a little backwards?"

"I know, I owe you an explanation. Here's the deal. There are some old investors who aren't involved in the company anymore, but we still have to honor our contract with them. Then we'll be free to move on and start releasing some real records, the stuff that will make us all millionaires. Thing is, we had promised them a certain number of songs, and we've just got to get those off our plate before we can legally go ahead with our real releases. You follow me?"

"I think so. We've got to satisfy an outstanding contract, so anything goes. Just bang the stuff out."

"Correct."

"Fine, no problem. One more question: just how many of these songs do we have complete in order to fulfill the contract?"

Ted looked at his clipboard, then looked at me.

"About three hundred."

3.

All day, every day, I was writing songs. When I finished one project I would come up with more song titles, invent a project name, then hit the keys and write songs to fit the titles. There was no time to wait for inspiration, there were too many songs to do. Ted hired a couple of other guys to help with the backlog of songs. They came in mostly at night, so I didn't see much of them, but they seemed nice enough.

I had complete freedom to do what I wanted. I made my own hours, and spent all day listening to music, messing around with the equipment, trying to write songs as fast as I could. I was listening to a lot of techno, hip-hop, and house music. I thought the best music would be made entirely by a computer, without any human intervention. I thought I was doing the next best thing. I only felt semi-human most of the time anyway.

Every couple of weeks Ted would ask for more song titles, then a group name, and then I would have to write the music. The titles I came up with were ridiculous: songs like "2069: A Sex Odyssey" and "Don't Pinch My Fanny 'til I'm Gone" were written for "groups" like Unformatted Brain, Geritol Rebellion, and The Round-Eye Rockers.

If it all seemed a little bit strange, I wasn't going to complain. I'd had some strange gigs before: my first music job had been writing music for porno movies. In the studio I actually had to improvise a solo guitar piece during one interminable blowjob sequence. I was seventeen. Then there was the hooker at Michigan State who once hired me to play guitar in the room while she took on an entire frat house, something like thirty guys in four hours. Or the trip to Montreal with the famous punk rocker, now dead, whose act included eating a box of laxatives and shitting on the stage. During the show the bouncers mistook me for a heckler and I got thrown off the stage at my own gig. There was also a pre-op transsexual who wanted to collaborate with me on a musical version of his/her sex change operation—this was years before

Hedwig—but then he/she got fresh and gave my balls a squeeze on Avenue A one night and that ended that. Besides, he had a stronger grip than I did.

Working at Monsieur didn't involve hookers, laxatives, crazy bouncers or frisky transvestites. I considered myself lucky.

4.

Most nights I went down to the Nail, and drank and sang songs until late. Usually, Anna was working and we'd play Yahtzee. But one night, during Anna's usual shift, Yvonne was working. Yvonne was an exchange student from Finland, studying at a local college for the semester. She didn't work too often, but when she did she would tell me how much she liked my playing and singing. She was nice to everybody. Every guy in the place was in love with her, especially Ben. Yvonne was tall and gorgeous, with long brown hair almost to her waist, and a sexy accent. She pronounced her name Ee-PHON.

This particular night, just before closing time, Yvonne came over to me.

"I have to ask you something. Would you walk me home tonight? I've had some problems recently."

"Sure, Yvonne, no problem."

She locked up and I walked with her down the street. After a few blocks she whispered, "Don't look now, but we are being followed." I looked. It was Ben. He looked drunk. But then, so was I. He was about a block behind us.

"See him?"

"Sure."

67

"He's the problem. He's been following me home every time I work, trying to ask me out."

"Don't worry, that's just Ben. He's harmless."

"He scares me."

When we got to her door Yvonne kissed me. Then she grabbed my hair and really kissed me. Her tongue darted in and out, then she pushed away.

"I'm sorry," she said, "but I told Ben I was seeing someone. He's standing over there, in the parking lot."

I looked again. She was right. It was definitely creepy.

"Would you mind coming in for a little while? It will look less suspicious that way."

We went upstairs and outside her door she put a finger to her lips.

"Don't make too much noise, my mother's visiting from Finland and she's asleep." We kissed again. Yvonne began grinding against me, moaning softly and slipping back into her maddening accent.

"You have *safed* me tonight, you *safed* me!"

Yvonne had a small studio apartment, the bed was in the middle of the living room and there was a kitchenette off to the side. From the light streaming in the window I could see her mother curled on one side of the bed. She looked as good as Yvonne. Maybe better.

"Let's go in the bathroom."

"Hell no, let's wake mom up too."

Yvonne shushed me and tugged my arm. She thought I was joking.

We went into the bathroom and Yvonne pulled off her tight top, unsnapped her bra, and two glorious firm mounds bounced to attention. I sucked on her hard little nipples and began feeling

68

under her skirt. Then she sat on the toilet seat and undid my pants and began sucking me off. I was sorry I'd had that last beer. Yvonne stood up and shimmied out of her panties. She leaned over the toilet and presented the rump. She was all legs and ass, and was in such good shape she could bend all the way down, so her hands were on the floor. I grabbed her haunches and slid into that furry little bush. It was hard, fast, and brutal. Her breath came out in short bursts, she was trying not to make noise. I reamed and poked and jabbed. What is it about nurses? I thought. I was in the wrong career.

When it was over Yvonne put her panties and bra back on and we tiptoed into the living room. Yvonne pointed to a little couch against the wall.

"You don't have to go home so late. You can sleep there."

I slept there.

In the morning Yvonne and her mother were already up. They had fixed breakfast and coffee, and had even set a place for me. Yvonne introduced me to her mother. I was right, she was a fox. Breakfast was awkward, until Yvonne's mother broke the silence.

"So Ee-PHON, you two haf a good night?"

"We didn't do much, just hanging out at the bar."

"I mean, did you haf a nice time in ze bathroom?" Her mother winked at me. "You see," I cried, "I told you we should have woken her up!" Her mother began to laugh, then Yvonne and I did too.

69

5.

I saw Yvonne only once after that. She acted like she didn't know me. Then she went back to Finland. Ben was heart-broken. For that matter, so was I. Then I met Stacy.

It was a hot and muggy night, and I was sitting in the Nail having a cold pint when a woman took the stool next to mine. She looked young, not even old enough to drink. She was wearing a lot of makeup, as if to make herself look older, but it had the opposite effect. She got on her toes and leaned over the bar and ordered a soda, then turned to me.

"Say you're with me."

"You're with me," I said.

"I mean it," she said. She looked scared. "If he comes in here, say you're with me. "Who?" "My ex-husband. He just tried to rape me, because I wouldn't give him money to buy drugs. I barely got away from him. If he comes in here, say we're together, okay?" "No way," I said. "I'm not looking for trouble." "Great." She sat down on the stool. I went back to drinking my beer. A few minutes went by. Every time the door opened she would jump. After ten or fifteen minutes she began to relax. "He would have been here by now. He probably went to get more drugs and booze and has already forgotten. I'm sorry I put you on the spot like that."

"It's okay."

She bought me a beer, and we started talking. Her name was Stacy, and she had a sad story to tell. She was 22, and had two kids by her ex-husband, aged 2 and 4. Stacy had lost custody, and the kids were living with her ex-husband's mother. Her own mother wanted nothing to do with her.

"I've been clean and sober for six months now, and I can barely even see my kids, but my ex-husband can drive drunk and get coked up and try to rape me and he's around them all the time, the judge thinks I'm the bad parent. It pisses me off."

Stacy kept saying how she was going to get her kids back, that she would not rest until she got them back, she was never going to touch another drug or drink. I'd heard similar stories before, but there was something about Stacy that made me believe her. It's easy to tell when a drug addict is lying, you can tell if someone's been high recently or is still using. Stacy had a lot of fire but she was very cool too, calm and in control of herself. She was short, with a slim body, and feathered light brown hair that was parted in the middle and spilled down over her shoulders. Her face was kind of plain, but I thought she was cute.

We talked for a long time. When Stacy got up to go to the bathroom, Anna came over to me.

"Watch out for that one," she warned in her Irish accent, "she's a bad one. Fucking bitch."

"I don't know," I said, "I think she's nice."

Anna snorted. "Nice? What kind of cunt abandons her kids just so she can be some alkie slut?" Anna threw her head back and walked haughtily down to the end of the bar. I followed her with my eyes. Stacy came back from the bathroom. "Let's get out of here," I said.

We went outside. "Do you have a car?" she asked. I pointed to my truck and we went over and got in.

"Where to? Where do you live?"

Stacy shook her head. "I can't go there. The place I'm living has strict rules, and I missed curfew. Nobody is admitted after 11p.m. unless you have permission in advance."

"Are you going to get in trouble?"

71

"No, it's not a big deal. The only thing I'm worried about is my job. I was on public assistance, but I just got a job. If I get fired I'll be screwed, the courts want to see you can provide for your children."

"You're welcome to stay at my place," I said, "but I have to warn you. It's pretty grim."

Stacy thought for a moment. "That's okay," she said. "Grim's good."

My bed was narrow, and we pressed ourselves together and entwined our legs. Stacy's lips were soft, she was a great kisser. She was wearing some kind of fruit-flavored lip gloss, which reminded me of high school, and those parties on the golf course, and why I wanted to be a musician in the first place. Neil Young had sung about welfare mothers. He was right. I thought Anna had completely misjudged her, but still, there was something about Stacy that I didn't completely trust. We gave each other a good ride, then drifted off to sleep.

In the morning when I woke Stacy was gone. The weak buttery sun was filtering through the dirty curtains. I turned off the alarm. I thought maybe Stacy was in the bathroom, but then I noticed that all her belongings were gone, her clothes and jacket and pocketbook. I jumped out of bed and grabbed my pants. My money and wallet were still there. I looked out the window. The truck was there. I heard the door opening behind me and I turned.

It was Stacy, carrying a brown bag. She smiled at me. "I was hoping I'd make it back before you woke," she said.

"The alarm just went off. Where were you?"

She sat on the bed and started pulling things out of the bag. "I walked down the hill to the 7-11. I don't know how you like your coffee, but I got cream and sugar on the side. Here's some bottled water, too. It's good after you've been drinking. And I got you an orange juice, because you should have your vitamin C. Oh, and speaking of healthy, I got you more cigarettes, because I smoked a lot of yours last night."

"No you didn't."

"After you fell asleep I did," she said. I saw the ashtray on the floor, filled with butts. I sat next to her on the bed. "That coffee looks good," I said. She handed me one, and we clicked cups.

We finished our coffees, then I got dressed and grabbed the keys and drove Stacy to work. We were quiet for a while. It was a beautiful summer morning.

"Will I see you again?"

"I hope so," she said. "Things are pretty hard for me right now. I don't even have my own phone, and you can't call the house, because if they think I'm out with men they'll use it against me. They'll do anything they can to keep me from my kids. I know what they say about me, people like Anna. Everyone thinks I'm some kind of whore. It's not true."

"I believe you," I said.

"I'll call you when I can, and we'll try to get together. But I can't promise anything. Is that all right?"

"That's fine," I said. We pulled up to her job, it was a factory. There was a lunch truck in the parking lot. It made me nostalgic. "What do I owe you for the coffee?" I asked. Stacy clucked. "Nothing, silly. That's for being such a gentleman last night. Nobody's treated me that nice in as long as I can remember." She leaned over and kissed me. I kissed back. It was nice. I gave her my number, then she hopped out of the truck and jog-skipped over the asphalt, her feathered hair bouncing over her denim jacket. She looked back one more time and smiled and waved. I knew how she felt. Nobody had ever brought me breakfast before.

6.

I didn't hear from Stacy for about a week. Then one Saturday morning I got a call from her while I was still in bed. She was calling from a pay phone. She sounded excited.

"I can't believe it, but that nasty mother-in-law of mine actually is letting me see my daughter today! She doesn't have to, it's not my visitation day, but I asked her and she said yes! I'm so psyched!"

"That's great," I said. "What are you going to do?"

"There's a new movie out my daughter wants to see, it's down at the Quad. My son's too young, but I'm going to take my baby girl. We're going to the early show, then I have to send her right back. I asked if I could take her out for ice cream afterwards but the bitch said no. Still, it's better than nothing. It's silly, but I had to call and tell you. I can't wait!"

I laughed. "Have a great time."

I got up after a little while, then bought the newspaper and a coffee down at the 7-11. I checked the movie times. It was easy to figure, there weren't many movies a child that young could see. Then I went to the library and killed a few hours. When it was time I drove over to the theatre and pulled into a corner of the parking lot, in view of the door.

After ten minutes or so people began coming out of the theatre. Families, mostly. Stacy was short, so she was hard to spot, but eventually I saw her, holding her daughter's hand.

They were talking and laughing. I saw an older woman get out of a car. Stacy hugged and kissed the girl, then the older woman took the child and drove away. Stacy was standing there. I waited until the other car was gone, then pulled around and came alongside her. Stacy saw me and looked puzzled. I rolled down the window.

"Want to get an ice cream?" I asked her. Stacy grinned and got in the truck. Then she put her head in her hands and started sobbing.

7.

I don't remember the first time I heard the name Bert Slake, but suddenly it was all anybody at Monsieur could talk about: Bert Slake was coming! Bert Slake was going to work with us! The great Bert Slake!

I pulled Ted aside. "Who the hell is Bert Slake?" I asked. He rolled his eyes.

"He's only just about the biggest pop music producer in the world at this point, that's all! He's coming by to meet everybody, and to listen to the stuff we've all been working on! Do you know how huge this is? Izzy set all this up! I told you, Izzy is a genius!" Ted was beside himself, I'd never seen anybody so excited.

I found out more about this Slake character. It was true: he was a hot shit, had sold millions of records, and worked with some big names, mostly pop-dance divas. He was a heavyweight in the industry, the type of guy who could put us over. Monsieur had arrived.

We had a few weeks to put our best songs together for Bert Slake. It was exciting. I had learned a lot over the months, and my new material was better, more accomplished than anything I had done before. I was listening to a lot of house music, the deeper

75

the better. Kerri Chandler had just released *A Basement, a Red Light, and a Feeling,* and I listened to a lot of Murk Records, Ten City, Todd Terry, Masters At Work. It was a long trip but I went into the city more, and hung around the dance clubs, mostly the smaller, predominantly gay places that spun the best music.

Ted began working on a new song to present to Bert Slake. In the past Ted hadn't done much composing. Ted hated dance music. He had mocked it relentlessly the whole time I had been at Monsieur. He was still very much a hard rock guy, he still wanted to be a guitar god. His car was filled with Zeppelin bootlegs, and he had a picture of Jimmy Page hanging in his office.

Almost overnight, Ted began to change. I went into his office one day and noticed that the Zeppelin and Skynyrd posters had been taken down. He cut his hair, in what I guessed was a bid for a more "contemporary" look from the long, hard rock mane he'd always favored. It came out looking more like a short, permed mullet. His car stereo, which had once blared a constant barrage of classic rock, was now tuned to the local dance-pop station exclusively.

We were driving to the deli one day, Ted was blasting the radio, when a particularly offensive song came on the air. I don't remember the artist, but at some point the singer, in a husky, cloying alto warbled, "If loving you is wro-yo-yong, I don't want to be ri-yi-yight..."

I slapped the dashboard in disgust. It wasn't like Top 40 was generally known for its lyrical brilliance, but couldn't they do better than that tired old line? It was depressing.

"Jesus," I groaned, "that's fucking brilliant."

"I know," Ted answered softly, "totally." I looked over at him. He was staring off into the middle distance, nodding. He was serious.

Ted became obsessed with working on his new song. Ted's songs had always been the source of private jokes among the composers. They were full of outdated orchestrations, hackneyed vocals, insipid lyrics. He worked hard on them, but for all the effort, I just didn't hear anything. Sometimes while I'd be standing there one of the other composers would walk by and we'd look at each other and just shake our heads. It wasn't snobbery, it was just that all the time and money in the world couldn't hide the fact that Ted's heart just wasn't in it. He wanted fame and fortune, but he wasn't being true to himself. That was what made listening to his songs so painful. I didn't know what the hell I was doing either, but at least I loved the music I was trying to write. I actually knew what Motown was all about.

Ted could sense the negative reaction to his work. He became withdrawn, aggressive, distracted. He began throwing his weight around, snapping at people, making every-body's life more difficult. Ted would block out the best studios for days at a time, making it impossible for the rest of us to work. He hired a small army of professionals, at company expense: mixing engineers, keyboardists, percussionists, singers. In the past I would drop by whatever room Ted was working in, and sometimes he'd ask me to help him lay down some tracks, or give him my opinion on something. Now, whenever I walked in he'd snap at me and shoo me out.

Izzy had hired two guys from the New York dance scene to help promote Monsieur. Their names were C-Bo and Andre. They had asked to hear all the songs first, before Bert Slake came in. They had a lot of experience and knew what would sell in the market. I picked my best song, a simple, soulful house track with an amazing singer who had been recommended by one of the other composers. The music was still raw but it had a great per-

77

formance and a big hook. I had heard the songs the other guys were working on and felt good about mine, I thought it was the best thing being presented. If C-Bo and Andre liked it then there was a good chance that Bert Slake would like it too. Buzz. It was all about creating buzz. Someone had to do it, and Ted certainly wasn't going to. By then there was no way to avoid Ted's song, it was impossible not to hear snippets bleeding out of the studios. It sounded terrible, just a generic rhythm and some screechy nonsense on top. It was embarrassing. We all turned in cassettes of our songs, and tried to focus on our other work while we waited to hear what C-Bo and Andre thought.

Everybody was really excited for a few days. We would high-five each other as we passed in the hallways, there was a sense that good things were going to start happening.

Then Ted called a meeting.

The composers gathered in my room, on the leather sectional.

"I've got good news and bad news," Ted said. "The good news is, Bert Slake is very excited about coming to Monsieur and meeting everybody!" There was a cheer.

"So what's the bad news?" someone asked.

"There's been a little change in plans," he said. "I hate to tell you guys this, but Bert Slake has decided that rather than listen to a bunch of different material, he's more interested in seeing what kind of united front we can show, to see how well we work together. What that means is, we can only present him with one song, and the rest of you guys will do a remix of that song."

I raised my hand. "And, uh, what song would that be?" Ted smiled.

"Well, at the meeting it was decided that my song was the best chance we had for a hit single."

You could feel the air leave the room. Shoulders and heads slumped. Jimmy, one of the other composers, spoke up.

"So, this song of yours, this big top-secret project. Are you going to tell us the name, or will you then have to kill us all?" Ted pulled out a cassette. He laughed, nervously.

"Of course I can tell you. I'm going to play it for you now. It's called 'If Loving You Is Wrong'."

8.

All the excitement that had been building at Monsieur was gone. The place went from being a party to a morgue overnight. We each got tapes of "If Loving You Is Wrong." The song was a piece of shit. I went to the back offices, where the marketing guys were. I went over to C-Bo's desk.

"Look, C-Bo," I said, "I respect you, I know your taste in music is good. So how could you guys pick Ted's track to play for Bert Slake?"

C-Bo shook his head. "I'm sorry, man, it wasn't me. I tried. The meeting was a joke. It was like Ted and Izzy had already decided everything before we got in there. Actually, we really liked your song, with that great vocalist."

"Thanks."

"Izzy just kept saying that Ted was his boy, and he was going to stand behind him all the way. Izzy's the boss, he signs the checks, so that was that. It wasn't like they were asking our opinion, they were just telling us."

"That's what I figured."

Nobody wanted to touch Ted's track. It was like having to tie two blenders filled with tin cans to your ears. As a result, the other

79

composers made only minor changes—a new drum loop here, some sound effects there. They were just too disgusted to put any real effort into it.

The more I thought about the situation, the angrier I got. I was going to pull out of the project altogether, but that would have only hurt me in the end. If I had to hear that song, knowing I had copped out, I would hate myself.

I told Ted I needed the main studio for the weekend. When I told him it was so I could work on "If Loving You Is Wrong," he seemed pleasantly surprised. "That's my boy," he said, slapping me on the back. "Make me proud."

You have no idea, I thought.

That Saturday I came in with two six-packs and a bag of weed. I had the place to myself. I rolled a fat joint, smoked half, and got to work.

I worked from scratch, using none of Ted's original track. Instead I threw together all the strangest sounds I could find. Where he was fast, I went slow. Where he was high, I went low. I spent several hours working just on the bass sound, layering and adjusting it until it was an ominous, subsonic rumble. The only parts of the original track that I used were some of the verses and the ad-libs, the singer's yelps and cries. I completely ignored the chorus, which hit new depths of poetic depravity: "If loving you is wrong/then come on baby let's be wrong all night long/we can make sweet love all through the night/come on baby I don't wanna be right!"

I made my own kind of sweet love all through the night, fucking his track.

In the morning I was done. I made a cassette of the mix and slid it under Ted's door, then got drunk for two days. When I came back to work Ted called me into his office. He asked me to close the door. He put on a tape. It was my remix. It sounded even better than I had remembered. Ted didn't know how lucky he was to have me there, to make him look good. A minute into the track Ted stopped the tape deck.

"Is this some kind of joke?"

"What?"

"This sounds like fucking shit! At first I thought you had recorded the whole thing in reverse!"

I steadied myself. Keep your cool, I thought. Remember who it is you're talking to.

"Look, Ted, the whole point of doing a remix is to create a different mood, to blow people's minds. The way to break into the clubs is with something like that—something dark and nasty, completely off the wall."

"But you didn't even use the lyrics! That's the whole *point* of the song, the whole heart and soul of it!"

"A bunch of stoned club kids don't give a flying fuck about lyrics when they're flailing around a dance floor at six in the morning, high on ecstasy."

"Don't try to jive me, Hall, I know you're good with words!"

I threw up my hands and walked out.

The day of the Bert Slake presentation Ted was like a school-girl on prom night. He preened and fussed, arranged and rearranged the chairs in the studio at least ten times, barked orders at all of us. When it was time, we shuffled into the room. Ted asked me to work the tape machine.

Bert Slake was a big guy, with a long train of hair down his back. He carried a silver-tipped cane and wore a jaunty driving cap. He brought his assistant with him, a squeaky-looking guy in a black turtleneck with an affected English accent.

The first track was Ted's version of "If Loving You Is Wrong." It sounded even more horrible than I remembered. It actually seemed to get worse every time I heard it. It was pure cheese, relying on a sort of grating, high-energy Latin sound that had been popular a few years earlier. The whole sound was frantic and stale, with dated drums, canned staccato piano and those infernal orchestra hits that were so overused at the time, which sounded like gorillas farting into steel drums.

Everybody listened to the track in silence. The tension in the room was as thick as the cheese coming out of the monitors. When the song was finally over the great Bert Slake raised his head.

"Too dated. That style's over. Next."

Ted's face dropped, and all the other composers looked uneasy. I think that's when it finally hit them: that by making their versions barely different from the original, they had lashed themselves to Ted. They were going to go down in flames just as hard.

A few bars into the first remix Bert Slake signaled me to stop the tape.

"Isn't this the same number?" he asked. "I thought I was going to hear a lot of different songs!"

We all glared at Ted.

"Oh, well, that was the *original* plan," he explained hastily, motioning to the rest of us. "But then we all decided that, you know, it would be better to show a *united* front. You know, get behind the best song we had to offer!"

Bert Slake rolled his eyes, and motioned for me to roll the tape. Ted had a frozen grin on his face, he wouldn't make eye contact with any of us.

The next few minutes seemed like hours. Mix after mix came on, each one practically identical to the last. Bert just kept shaking his head, and motioning to me to skip to the next track.

My mix was last. When it was about to start Ted made a move like he was going to turn off the tape machine. I blocked his wrist.

It started with steely background chatter, representing Ted's doubletalk and inanity. Then I added reverse cymbal splashes and faint horn echoes—the sound of the cavalry bugles blowing over the windswept deserts of ignorance! Then a dirty, subsonic bass line that rumbled the floor, representing the unleashed Id, rising up from the sands of time to overwhelm the oppressors. I was a student of King Tubby, Adrian Sherwood, and the Bomb Squad. Finally the singer's voice, processed and haunting, came stabbing out from the middle of the confusion, swirling from one speaker to the other.

The chattering grew louder, the cymbals more ominous, then a gurgling rumbling orgasmic rushing up into a big dirty kick drum punching through the middle: BOOM, BOOM, BOOM, BOOM-BOOM-BOOM, BOOM, BOOM....

Ted clapped his hands and tried to say something. Bert raised his hand and Ted slunk back into the shadows.

Apart from Ted's version, mine was the only one Bert listened to completely. All seven glorious minutes of it. When it ended the mighty Bert Slake looked around the room.

"Who did that last track?"

"I did," I said.

"Excellent," he said, standing up. "That's the one, that's the sound you're looking for. It's got that real club sound, which is the direction you should be going in. Don't chase the pop charts, you'll never get anywhere that way. Go for the clubs, the underground. Like that last track."

I felt something on my back. It was Ted's hand.

"Yeah," Ted said, grinning. "I knew you'd like that one, that's why I saved it for last."

Bert and his assistant thanked everybody and left, with Ted holding open the door and bowing. He followed them out, babbling. Nobody said anything. A moment later the door opened. Ted stuck his head into the room and grinned at us.

"Well, what are you all waiting for? You heard the man, people...let's club it up!"

9.

Underground! It was Ted's new buzzword. Everything had to be Underground! I would walk by his office and hear him on the phone: "You see, I really consider myself a club guy, I'm really into the *underground* sound...." It made me sick.

Suddenly, tracks Ted had raved about in the past he now pooh-poohed for not being *underground*, songs composers were working on he criticized as not sounding *underground* enough. He listened to my remix over and over, I could hear it coming out of his office. He had to have it, he needed to own that sound. After blowing me off for a month, Ted was my best buddy again.

10.

Ted wasn't the only one who wanted to horn in on my act. Pedro and Karl, the two technicians who kept the equipment running, said they wanted to write songs too. Since there were still plenty of songs to write for the investors, Ted agreed. He asked me to work with them.

The next afternoon I started working with Pedro. As soon as the door to the composing room was closed, Pedro began pacing the floor and complaining bitterly about Ted.

"I know he's your friend, Tim, but as far as I'm concerned, Ted's a racist."

I had come up with many names for Ted in recent days, but racist wasn't one of them.

"What do you mean?"

"Look, no offense, but all the composers here are white guys. Except for you, none of the other guys even *like* this music, they don't listen to it or go to clubs or anything!"

It was true. I didn't know what to say.

"Blacks and Latinos created this music, but a Puerto Rican guy like me can't get a chance in this place."

"Aren't you getting a chance now?"

Pedro ignored me. He shook his head. "I'm telling you, it's racist." Then he got up and put on his jacket.

"Where are you going? I thought we were going to write some songs!"

"I can't, I have to get home. My neighbors have been leaving garbage all over the sidewalk. There have been rats, bugs. It's disgusting. I'm finally having a meeting with them."

"Okay, good luck. Hope it works out."

"I doubt it," he said.

85

"Why not?"

Pedro shook his head.

"They're Dominican. Dominicans are all dirty people."

The next day Ted paired me up with Karl. Karl was the oldest of us, about forty. He was a decent mixing engineer, but for every five minutes he worked he took a ten-minute cigarette break. I'd never seen anything like it. Karl would sit at the keyboard, push a few buttons, then stop.

"Just one minute, doctor," he'd drawl, then amble out. Smoking was forbidden in the studios, so he'd puff away in the hallway, then grind the thing out and amble back in. Punch a few buttons, turn a few knobs.

"Hold the line, professor." And he'd be off again.

Between smoke breaks he talked to his girlfriend. They talked constantly during the day. There was always a drama, the woman was always having some sort of crisis at work. Karl's voice would rise in indignation at each new outrage.

"Now cupcake, you just tell those people....how DARE that woman!....don't cry, sweetness...." Every so often he would look at the clock, and break off the call: "I've got to go, cupcake, I've got work to do, but I'll call you back as soon as possible!" Then he'd run outside and have a cigarette.

It went on like that for a few weeks, Pedro complaining about how everybody always tried to keep a Puerto Rican down, and Karl talking his girlfriend down off the ledge between smoke breaks. Then they both gave up and went back to sitting sullenly in the tech room, grumbling over their soldering irons.

11.

I saw Stacy only occasionally. Sometimes she called but usually there would be a soft knock on my door in the evening and she would come in and we'd sit and talk and smoke. She was still working at the factory, she was trying to get her own place. I would tell her about Monsieur, and how I hoped to get my songs released some day. I would play her tapes of what I was working on, and then we would go to bed. In the morning I would drive her to work. She said her boss was hard on her, because he knew her situation, but that she was making the best of it. I admired her determination, and I told her so.

I was working on a new song one afternoon when the receptionist buzzed and said I had a call. It was Stacy, she was calling from the hospital. "It's nothing to worry about," she said. "I'm more bored than anything."

I left work early and went down to the hospital. I gave the name and room number at the front desk and they let me up. On the way over I had bought flowers, a book of crossword puzzles, comic books, anything I could think of.

I wasn't prepared for what I saw. Stacy looked terrible. She had circles under her eyes, and her skin had a sickly blue tone. Her lips were chapped. She gave a weak smile when she saw me. "I knew you'd come," she said softly. "My own mother didn't."

I sat by the bed and asked her what was wrong. She said it was an abdominal infection of some kind, and they were still doing tests. After about half an hour she got very tired and said she needed to rest. I kissed her and she thanked me for coming down, and I left.

The next day I called the hospital and asked for Stacy. "Who?" the person on the phone asked. I repeated the name and gave the room number. "I have no record of anybody here by that name," the woman said. "There must be a mistake," I said. "I saw her just yesterday. Did she check out?" "I can't give out that information," the woman replied. "Are you family?" "No, a friend." "I'm sorry, I can't give you any information."

I hung up. I didn't know what to do. The only thing I really knew about Stacy was where she worked, and I knew she wouldn't be going back there anytime soon, the way she had looked. I figured she would call or stop by when she could. I hoped she was all right.

I had other things to worry about. One night Ted asked me to stay after work, to help him with a special project. When the others had left for the night I followed him into the back office. It was Ted, the office manager, and me. There a box filled with cassettes, a roll of clear plastic film, and a hair dryer.

I pulled out one of the cassettes. It was professionally printed, like a cassette you would buy in a store. Except on the side of this tape it said "Big-Eyed Beans From Venus." The first track on Side A was "Beige Pumps."

Ted pulled it out of my hand. "Don't touch that," he barked.

"Those are my songs!"

"Look," he said, "the reason I asked you here is because I trust you, okay? Nobody else can know about this, okay?"

"What's going on?"

"I'll level with you. The investors are not very happy with us right now. It was a miscommunication, really, but they were under the impression that we were actually going to release these songs commercially."

"How silly of them."

"See, they got wind of our connection with Bert Slake, so now they want a piece of it. Izzy's working on the details so everybody will wind up happy. But we have to get these cassettes packaged and over to FedEx by 9:00. Let's get started."

There were about sixty cassettes in all, a dozen copies each of five different "albums". There were printed paper cards, which had to be folded and inserted into the clear plastic boxes, and we set up an assembly line, putting the inserts into the boxes, then the cassettes, then moving them down the line to the plastic film, which had to be cut to size. The last step was with the hair dryer, to individually shrinkwrap each tape. Shrinkwrapping was the hardest part, it was easy to melt through the plastic and I ruined many before one of the girls took the hair dryer. Then it went smoothly.

We finished with less than fifteen minutes to spare, and we carried the packages out to the office manager's car and she took off for FedEx. Ted kept saying that it was just a technicality, that there was really nothing to it, that this was just a bump in the road and it would all work out. I wasn't so sure.

I had never seen a car peel out of a parking lot so fast.

I kept thinking about Izzy Klein. Izzy was the owner and founder of Monsieur Records. I hardly ever saw him. He was a young guy, a former musician, and he seemed nice enough. He lived in one of the most exclusive parts of Long Island, one of those North Shore enclaves so wealthy that they had no street lights or signs, and the roads were hardly paved. I believe there was actually a committee to prevent such improvements. The idea was to make it look like it was still a rustic, rural community, and not a green and pretty prison of murderers, thieves, and con men.

The Kleins had thrown some lavish parties. People would stand around drinking fine wine out of good crystal, and marvel at the house, the cars, the jewelry. Izzy's wife, Janine, was a plump young thing who strutted around with a big blonde bouffant, sparkly fuchsia lipstick, and bright red, two-inch fake nails. She was a true Long Island princess, who had found her prince and now lived in her palace, with two Jaguars in front and a large swimming pool out back. "Investments," she would say proudly to all who asked, "Izzy made it all with investments. He's a financial genius!"

I finally understood. It didn't take a rocket scientist to figure it out, and I supposed I should have seen it earlier. The "investments" she had bragged about were really the millions that the investors had pumped into Monsieur over the years. The Kleins had used the money to build Monsieur, while furnishing an obscenely lavish lifestyle for themselves. The investors had gotten Big-Eyed Beans From Venus.

12.

A few nights later I was at the Nail. Anna came over. "Too bad about your friend," she said.

"What? Oh yeah," I said. "I visited her in the hospital, she looked pretty bad. Some kind of abdominal infection."

"Is that what she called it?" Anna snorted. "That's a hell of a way to put it."

"What are you talking about?"

Anna looked surprised. "Didn't you hear? Stacy's dead." She was about to say something else, then she saw my look. "Oh God, I'm sorry," she stammered.

"Anna, you're a fucking cunt," I said. I got up and left.

I took a week off from work. I stayed in my room, and only left to get more beer and cigarettes at the 7-11. I kept thinking about that first night, and the orange juice and coffee and water the next morning. I thought about her lip gloss, and her lips, and the kids. She was a good person. I was so sick of things not being fair.

I went back to work but it hardly mattered. The company was going down, fast. Monsieur was a war zone. Every few days Ted would race through the studios, giving people orders: "If anybody comes in and asks you any questions, don't say anything!" Scowling men, wearing suits and carrying briefcases, would come through the studios, talking softly and walking briskly. Nobody looked happy. Izzy started showing up at the offices more and more. Sometimes on my way in or out I could hear him screaming over the telephone from his office all the way in the back.

People started taking off for other companies, including C-Bo. "I'm getting out while I can," he said. "You should come with me, I'm sure we could find you someone to put out your tracks. You've got talent." "Thanks," I said, "but I think I'll stick around and see what happens." "Suit yourself, man.

But if you ever come out to Brooklyn, look me up."

Ted said that we still had to fulfill our contract to the investors, so I kept working on tracks. Every day it became more and more apparent that Monsieur, at the most fundamental level, was really a scam. I wasn't so angry about that, because I was used to that in the music business, but because Ted had been so willing, so eager, to step over the rest of us in order to get ahead. It was like the guy who runs you off the road and then slams into a brick wall a block later—you can't help but feel a bit smug.

Ted was constantly in meetings, he looked worried and haggard where he had once been full of cocky bravado. We were forbidden to ask questions. That was okay, because I didn't plan on asking any. I started taking long, leisurely lunch breaks. I had found another bar closer to the studio and would stop there for a beer and sometimes not bother going back to work.

It was after one of my three-hour lunches at the bar and I was in the composing room, resting my head on a Roland keyboard. It was dim, and cool, and I was playing the *Let's Do It Again* soundtrack on the Technics. Curtis Mayfield and the Staple Singers. You couldn't beat it. Ted came in quietly and closed the door.

"I've got some bad news, Tim. I have to let you go."

I didn't say anything.

"It's not just you, it's all the composers. Except for Paul. He's been here the longest. We're going to try to save the company, with some new songs. If it works out, I'd like to hire you back."

Paul was a tall geek who wore a tie to work every day. What he could do to help the company, I didn't know. He wrote jazzy pop, rinky-dink little numbers that sounded like the kind of music they would play on a carousel at a theme park for child molesters.

Then again, he wouldn't be any competition for Ted, either.

"I understand," I said.

"Thanks for all you've done. Sorry it didn't work out."

I spent the rest of the afternoon getting my stuff together and loading the truck: guitars and amps, effects pedals, records and tapes. It was a sweet job; I was going to miss it. Ted didn't waste any time, he was already in my room, working on another project. It took me a moment to realize that it was a new version of "If Loving You Is Wrong," done in an "underground" style. It was a grotesque parody of my remix. Except that Ted, as always, had gotten it wrong. His version was filled with the same ugly orchestrations and outdated sounds that ruined all his work. Every time I walked by and heard it my right eyebrow would begin to twitch.

I did a final check in all the rooms, to make sure I wasn't forgetting anything. I went back into the composing room. Ted had stepped out. I saw a notebook next to the computer that looked like the kind I used, so I picked it up and flipped through it. It was Ted's notebook, and it was filled with a lot of song lyrics and self-help jargon. Stuff about seizing the day and living in the moment. On one page, in a childlike hand, Ted had written "Learn French," and under that had listed his reasons:

1. *so I can say "Monsieur" right*
2. *to order wine in restrants and impres chicks*
3. *improv my brian*

I stood there for a moment, I didn't know whether to laugh or cry. *Improv my brian.* It would have made a good song title. I put the notebook back, then went to accounting and told them where to mail my severance.

13.

I was lying in bed, trying to think of what to do. There was a knock on the door. I opened it and took a step back.
"Aren't you going to invite me in?"
She came in. Nicely dressed, new hairstyle.
"I heard you were dead."
"From who, that bitch Anna? Yeah, I heard she was telling people that. Wishful thinking. As soon as I heard I came right over. I didn't want you to worry about me."
"What does she have against you?"
Stacy sighed. "Her boyfriend. It's ridiculous. He's this big disgusting pig, a biker. Before I quit drinking I was a mess, and he kept asking me out. I slept with him once, but that was before

93

Anna was even going out with him. Turned out she was totally in love with him, but he ignored her until I told him I didn't want to see him again. Anyway, she keeps claiming I fucked her boyfriend, but it's bullshit. That's why she hates me."

"Why didn't you call me? The hospital wouldn't tell me anything."

"I'm sorry."

I sat down.

"Are you all right?"

"I am, actually, and that's the other thing I wanted to tell you. I met someone. He's very rich and he's madly in love with me." She jangled her keys. "I've got his Cadillac outside. Do you want to go for a drive?"

"No thanks."

"You're mad at me."

"I'm just glad you're all right. I was really upset."

"I'm so sorry, I really didn't think Anna would be such a bitch."

"Does he treat you well?" Stacy beamed. "Like a princess. I actually answered an ad he had, for a room to rent. He's got this big house down by the water. We got to talking and I realized he was a really good person."

"And rich."

Stacy kicked my right shoe. "That wasn't the reason, I swear. But he wants to help me get custody of my kids, he has this great lawyer and we're going to talk to him. He buys me clothes and lets me drive his car."

"Be careful."

"Yes sir," she said. She came over and knelt in front of me and took my hands. "Thank you for everything. You are one of the sweetest people I've ever met."

"I'm glad things are looking up for you."

"How's the music going? How's work?"

"Fine."

Stacy smiled. "Good, I'm glad. I want you to do great things with your music, I know you will someday. I got a new job recently. I'm learning how to type and use a computer. It's so much better than the factory." She looked at her watch.

"I don't want to leave, but I promised Phil I'd get the car back to him within the hour. He's a little possessive of me, it's really cute."

I walked her to the door. We kissed. Stacy put her arms around my neck and stood on her toes. We kissed again. "Go." She went.

A few nights later, drunk, I went back to Monsieur. What I was hoping to do, I can't recall—I think it involved scaling the roof, breaking in through an air vent, and robbing the place blind—but as I pulled up I noticed something strange. A bright orange sticker was stuck on the door. I got out of the truck and walked over. "This property has been sealed by the U.S. Marshall's Office. Trespassing is strictly forbidden.." There were official notices from the IRS, Revenue Canada, and several other agencies pasted alongside. That's when I noticed that there was a thick chain and padlock through the door handles. It must have been quite a show. I'd risk stealing from Monsieur Records, but not Uncle Sam. A light snow was beginning to fall. I had eighty-seven dollars in the bank and a hundred twenty thousand miles on the truck. Neither of us was going to make it to California. We probably wouldn't make it farther west than Brooklyn. Okay, then, Brooklyn it was.

Poopstain Magazine

Poopstain magazine was the brainchild of Jack Portabello, a young entrepreneur who'd made a fortune in the postcard printing business. In its four years of existence Poopstain had enraged more self-righteous celebrities, Christian Conservatives, and soccer moms—earning it more threats and lawsuits—than any other publication of its kind. Pornography, drugs, gore—nothing was off-limits, nothing was sacred. It was the hippest magazine in the country. I had every issue in a pile in the bathroom.

At the time, my current job wasn't going well. I wanted to leave, I just didn't have the ambition to look for work, repeat the whole stupid cycle over again. So when Jack, who knew me from a small local newspaper I used to run, asked me to step in as Poopstain Webmaster, I jumped at the chance. Poopstain magazine!

Jack flew me out to the Los Angeles office to discuss strategy. It was my first business trip. Jack's assistant picked me up at the airport in a shiny new Lexus. I looked out at the blinding

Los Angeles sunshine, the glorious palms, and I felt the whole possibility that was California. Settlers, prospectors, the dream of a better life. I was finally living it, my own dreams were finally coming true!

Still, nothing prepared me for the offices. Deluxe leather chairs, shiny new iMacs, burbling fountains, situated high atop a tower on Wilshire Boulevard that was just steps from the beach. The Santa Monica pier went off into the ocean, and the palm trees swayed while the famous California sun streaked across the sky and sank behind the ocean in a breathtaking finale of color and romance.

I stayed for a week of meetings, planning sessions, strategies. Unlike my old job, people were listening to my ideas, looking to me for guidance. I started to feel the Hollywood magic: I've made it, baby, I'm really somebody now, I'm on my way! Still, looking around, a part of me was nervous: could the magazine really be doing that well? I knew firsthand how hard it is to turn a profit in publishing. When I counted the ad pages, and counted how many staff were on the payroll, and took into consideration the printing costs for a glossy, four-color magazine, it didn't add up. Jack assured me we had funding for as long as it took to make it work, so I put it out of my mind. There seemed to be plenty of money in poop.

At the end of the week I came back to the New York offices, which were depressing and meager by comparison, and began looking for an assistant. It wasn't going to be easy. I was willing to train the person, but Jack would only pay about half the going rate. Luckily, one of the editors had a friend who loved the magazine and was looking for work. I met her and she seemed all right. Weird, but willing.

Her name was Chantal. Her ears were mutilated almost beyond recognition, stretched, plugged, and pierced. She had trouble speaking, because of the giant silver ball resting on her tongue, pierced through and fastened by a smaller ball on the bottom.

"What do you do?" I asked her.

"I'm a Dom."

"Excuse me?"

"A dominatrix. But I want to learn web design."

"I see."

"My girlfriend thinks I should have some kind of skill besides flogging old men."

"Your girlfriend?"

"You know, my lover."

I was taking notes on a yellow pad, even though it was gratuitous. I was desperate and we had no time to interview others. On the pad I wrote: "Dominatrix...lesbian ... SCORE!"

"You've got the job," I said, thinking: how cool. I was probably the only Webmaster in New York with a lesbian dominatrix for an assistant.

There was just one problem, something I didn't think of at the time. Doms are used to giving orders, not taking them.

The next day, Chantal showed up three hours late. She gave some excuse—something about a late call from an investment banker, a cat o' nine tails, and a tongue bath for her boots—then mumbled some insincere words of apology and walked over to her desk. She looked at her smaller, fabric office chair, and my larger, leather chair, and calmly switched them. Then she picked up the phone from my desk and plunked it down on hers. Then the lamp.

"Chantal?"

"Yes?"

"Can I ask you what you're doing?"

"Making myself comfortable!"

I walked over, put the phone and lamp back on my desk.

"Stand up," I told her.

"Why?"

"Just do it, please."

She stood up, and I wheeled my chair back and returned her fabric chair.

Her silver lisping ball bobbed furiously on her tongue. "I can't thit in that puny little thing! Ith not right for a woman of my...*thtature.*"

There's a common stereotype, at least in New York, that Asians are the hardest-working people on earth, and I guess I would have been inclined to agree. But whoever started that myth obviously never polled the lesbian-dominatrix contingent. Chantal talked for hours on the phone, and went for long, leisurely smoking breaks, sometimes an hour at a time. I'd have to search the offices, hunting her down. Usually I'd find her lounging in the production department, jawing with one of the designers. When I'd walk in she'd look up and purr with faint indignation, "Are you looking for me?"

After a while, I missed her absences less. Chantal was a chronic talker. All day, without stop, she had to have noise coming from that steel-encrusted mouth of hers. It was like a sickness, she couldn't control it. Diarrhea of the mouth. A case of the gabs. I've known several people with this problem, who were either terrified or incapable of silence.

When there was nobody to talk to, Chantal would talk to her computer monitor.

"Wha-a-a-t? What the—come on, you stupid machine! Yeah! Yeah yeah yeah! All right!"

"Chantal...CHANTAL!"

"What?"

"Please be quiet! I can't think!"

She'd be quiet for a minute, then it would start again: "Shit! Oh, you stupid...*why I oughtta*...Da-a-a-mn! What the...?"

Then she began fighting with her slave.

"Vinyl, damn it! What did that bitch say to you! She what?! Oh man, just for that you're coming over this weekend and cleaning my house! Did you hear me? *What?* She did what? You *liked* it? Oh boy, now you're cleaning my bathroom with a fucking toothbrush. And you're doing my laundry! Do you want to try for dinner, too?"

When she hung up she told me about her problems.

"Some other bitch is trying to steal Vinyl away from me! He said she was very aggressive and came on to him sexually."

"What do you care? You're a dyke!"

"What you have to understand is, Vinyl is my *slave*, he is literally my *property*. If another dom comes onto the scene and tries being aggressive with him, it's like she's stealing my car, or my computer! I won't stand for it!"

"A good slave is hard to find."

"You said it."

One day I walked in after lunch and the office had been turned into a dressing room. A tall, skinny bald man wearing knee-high rubber waders and a dog collar was kneeling at Chantal's feet, buffing her nails. Leather chaps, metal codpieces, rubber bras, littered the place. Chantal was reclining in my chair, on my phone, feet on my desk. I pressed my finger on the button.

"Why'd you do that?"

"Chantal, we have to talk."

"Wait! I want you to meet Vinyl, my slave. Vinyl, say hello to the great Poopstain webmaster!" Vinyl put down the nail file and bowed low to the ground.

I had to admit, I liked his style.

"Arise, my son." The geek rose.

"Vinyl is getting me ready for the big Dominatrix Ball tonight at Le Dungeon."

"That's what you think."

"Huh?"

"I mean, move it. Out. Now. Amscray."

Vinyl gathered up the rubber, leather, and metal studs and bowed and scraped and took himself and his big rubber waders out of there. I pulled my—I mean, Chantal's—chair over and sat down.

"Listen, Chantal, I know that even under the best of circumstances, work is work. It basically sucks. Also, I know we're not paying you much. That's why I'm trying to be understanding. But look, every time you walk in an hour late, or leave early, or sit and talk on the phone where others can see you, you make me look bad. And stupid or not, I need this job. I *like* it here. I don't care how you want to work but you can't make me look bad in the process. Am I making myself clear?"

She looked at me blankly.

"Okay, then let me put it to you this way. You are my *slave*, Chantal. My *property*. Understand? And if you don't shape up you'll be shining my shoes with your goddamn tongue!"

Chantal's mouth dropped open, her tongue ball quivered. But instead of telling me to fuck off, like I expected, she looked down and spoke in a quiet voice.

"Yeth thir," she said. "I underthtand."

Chantal got better after that. Which only meant she took

101

slightly less advantage than before. Still, it was an improvement. There were other things on my mind, some things I just couldn't figure out. The Los Angeles offices, for one. What was the point? There were ten people out there, full-time, although it didn't seem like the operation justified more than three. Plus, they had those big swank offices, the shiny new computers, the glorious sunsets. The whole Hollywood lifestyle. It was a good show but terrible business. And just who was Jack trying to impress? Porno stars and punk rockers? On quiet days I could hear the company's profits, and future, being sucked away.

There were other signs that the intricacies of running a bi-coastal operation were beyond Jack's reach.

On my first day I had noticed a small office near the front desk. The sign on the door said SPHINX. The door was usually closed, but when it was open I could see a lot of equipment and computers. There were two guys in the office. One of them would watch a little ball spin on the computer screen. He would click the mouse and the ball would spin. Click, spin. Click, spin. The other guy always seemed to be staring into a notepad, some-times for hours.

Finally I asked someone what their purpose was.

"Oh, those are the Sphinx boys. They're friends of Jack's, he lets them use that office. They're brilliant web designers. Jack's helping them get started in business, he bought all their equipment."

"They never seem to have any clients."

"They don't."

"How can that be, if they're so good?"

"They say it's because they're too expensive, most clients can't afford them."

"Why don't they lower their prices?"

"They say they're too good."

It was the riddle of the Sphinx—or the Sphinxters, as I came to call them. They were the only web designers I had ever met who were too good to have any clients.

One day one of them—the guy who spent all day clicking on the spinning ball—handed me something.

"We put out a magazine too," he said. "Here, check it out."

I went to a bar after work and read the thing. Sphinx magazine promised to be a "dangerous exploration into the inner reaches of the urban beast," but it was basic stuff: spelunking, climbing bridges, conspiracy theories—and all of it wrapped in a romantic, juvenile persecution complex that hinted at an overweening vanity: "There are over half a dozen government agencies monitoring us at all times...."

Big crap, I thought. My communist grandmother had twice that many watching her.

It seemed like every page had the word "manifesto" or "dossier" on it. It was unreadable garbage, so self-referential and self-conscious that it was unintentionally hilarious. "We have extensive files on the operational procedures of a dozen multinational corporations," they solemnly proclaimed. Sure, I thought, they're called annual reports. And when the Dragon Lady meets the one-armed man, the snow is deep in Pittsburgh.

They had given themselves titles like Minister of Information and Director of Operations. For subversives they sure liked dressing up in the titles of The Man. But it was all so they could remain anonymous, you see, one had to understand the danger. No, the Danger.

I found out the purpose of the little spinning ball. It was a special icon for their "highly classified" magazine. It seemed even an anti-government manifesto needed a slick corporate logo.

I would sit at my desk and wonder, Why does Jack put up with it? Why does he support a bunch of freeloaders who are spending his time and money putting out a competing product? Granted, their magazine could hardly be considered competition, but still. They should have been the ones putting the website together, gratis, in exchange for the free office space. Apparently Jack had suggested that once and they had flipped out. They were *too good*—even for Poopstain!

We plowed on. Chantal kept her phone calls and smoke breaks down, and even managed to come in on time occasionally. I was beyond caring. For a few weeks there was relative peace, though I knew: once the site was finished, so was she. It was something to look forward to.

When I got to the office that Monday before Christmas, I knew something was wrong. The office manager was locked in her office all morning, then she began calling in the editors one by one. When Bill, the managing editor, came in to talk to us, I knew it was over.

"I got some bad news, folks. We're shutting down."

Even though I was prepared for it, it hurt. Poopstain magazine, the best magazine in the country, maybe the world. Over?

"The ads just aren't there, and Jack's been covering the losses from his own pocket. We really tried, we just couldn't make it."

Bill went out to get beer and Chantal and I sat in stunned silence. I kept thinking about Jack's promise, that there was enough money for at least another year. It had been two months. I wondered if there wasn't a breach of contract in there somewhere. Fuck it. It hardly mattered. I heard a final, faint sucking sound in the West. Then Chantal spoke.

"I'm sad about the magazine, but in a way I'm pretty psyched!"

"Yeah, why's that?"

"For once I actually got laid off from a job. Usually I get fired!"

That afternoon the rest of us got drunk, and Chantal snuck out two hours early. I didn't care anymore. We had until the end of the week to get our stuff together, but when Chantal called in late the next morning, it was too much somehow. Even though we were lame ducks, and there was nothing to be done, I couldn't stand the thought of her taking advantage of me until the end, laughing her way into the unemployment lines. I waited until she got in, and listened to her lame excuse. I told her to get her stuff and get the hell out. It was a small consolation.

Jack called from L.A. and apologized. He said he was torn up about it.

"Everybody's gone here. There are just three of us. We're packing up the L.A. offices. We'll be working out of my apartment for a while. Hopefully we can rebuild. If I can get it together, would you still consider working with me? You were the best web guy we had."

"Sure, Jack."

By the end of the week, Bill and I were the only ones left. The beer flowed, the music played, and in the Sphinx office the little ball spun round and round and round. The postcard business was continuing, and so was Sphinx. I had no illusions about life being fair, but that burned me.

And just like that, the once-mighty Poopstain was gone.

When I got home the last night I was carrying a bag of groceries. My wife came into the kitchen as I began unpacking the stuff.

"Tonight," I said grandly, "I am cooking us a feast."

"That's sweet, dear, but wouldn't you rather go out? After all that's happened, I mean."

"It'll feel good to cook."

"Sure, it'll get your mind off it. What are you making?"

"Manifesto with clam sauce and a dossier salad."

"Oh, honey. You're really sad, aren't you?"

I kept my back to her and began quietly cutting the tomatoes.

Scumsquat Farewell

Dear Reader,

Well, it's finally here, after a two-year wait: the fifth and final issue of SCUMSQUAT. That's right, I'm sorry to announce the end of one of the most influential zines ever produced. It's certainly been a hell of a ride.

As some of you already know, there have been a number of legal and personal problems that have kept me from putting together this issue (mostly caused by my psycho ex-girlfriend, Janine...more about that later), but I'm here to say—no, shout!—that I WILL PREVAIL, and someday, though it may be a long time coming, JUSTICE WLL BE DONE.

It started in SCUMSQUAT #1, and the now-legendary "secret" photos of Janine giving me head in the kitchen at my mom's house (which inspired the name of the zine: SCUMSQUAT. Get it?) Only after I published the pictures did Janine claim she had no idea my video camera was on, which is TOTAL FUCKING BULLSHIT. Her only "proof" of this was that she hadn't signed a release form allowing me to use the photos, which is a fucking technicality and exactly the kind of sneaky thing she would do (I mean, she was MY GIRLFRIEND, what kind of "release" did I need besides the hot and creamy release that I shot down her throat, right?)

That first issue really put SCUMSQUAT on the map, and I sold out the entire 300 copies in a matter of months. I also garnered the prestigious "One To Watch in '99" award from the editors of You Ain't Zine Nothing Yet. Of course, this was back in the glory days of zines, not like these lame-ass losers doing it now, back when getting a "One To Watch" award was quite an honor, I assure you.

Jealous, petty jerk that she is, Janine was not amused, and she proceeded to write me a series of angry letters and left threatening messages on my answering machine (disproving her claim that she was the "innocent victim" in all this), which were reprinted in SCUMSQUAT #2 (which owing to the popularity of issue #1 was printed entirely on newsprint, with a color cover, 600 copies). This led to a number of ugly and almost violent confrontations between me and Janine at various coffee houses and clubs in Denver, after which Janine, trying to take the high ground, got a restraining order against me.

That led to my putting the groundbreaking (and, I should add, often imitated) "Wanted: Dead" poster in SCUMSQUAT #3 (the "Revenge" issue, an entirely ironic joke that was later misinterpreted by the prosecution), offering a five hundred dollar "reward" for anybody who would...well, you know. Of course this wasn't serious, but I realize in retrospect that this was a critical error. Because Janine, being the spiteful little monster she is, then went all legal on my ass and started proceedings against me.

Looking back, I probably shouldn't have also included her home address and phone number, or that two hundred dollar bonus for using a shotgun.

Things got so crazy that I decided to dedicate an entire issue of SCUMSQUAT to this remarkable, unfolding drama.

So for SCUMSQUAT #4, which I aptly called "The Confrontation Issue," I decided to record a face to face meeting with Janine, to get absolute proof that her claims that I was harassing, embarrassing, and stalking her were complete BULLSHIT, and also so we could put aside our problems once and for all. Because crazy as it may sound I still felt something for her, even if it was only a kind of twisted pity. Also, you know what they say about crazy women in bed, and I can tell you Janine was no exception. (But then, what else would you expect from a slut who once sucked my dick in my mom's kitchen? I mean, MY MOM'S FUCKING KITCHEN. 'Nuff said.) In fact, I wanted re-con-ciliation between us so much that I was even willing to apologize to the stupid bitch. Besides, the lawyer's fees had made me completely broke and I was hoping to make her see the light that this was a useless and destructive path she was on.

SCUMSQUAT #4 was also meant to be the first Brian Smelt Legal Defense Fund issue, and I was really excited about it. I got my friend Barry to boost his dad's video camera for the night (having already sold mine to pay for lawyer fees. Thanks, Janine), and then we smoked a nice fatty and drove in Barry's Chevette over to Janine's place. Barry got into position with the camera behind the bushes by her front door and I rang the bell. Janine came to the door. She was not happy. In fact, she was downright rude and nasty. She wouldn't talk to me, and reminded me I was violating the restraining order. I asked why she had to be, yes, such a fucking bitch all the time and why couldn't we just talk it out like reasonable adults? Unfortunately, that was when Barry lost his footing behind the bushes and made a noise and Janine totally nailed him. Busted!

Well, she tried to slam the door but I got my foot inside just enough and pushed my way in. I had no way of knowing, of course, that Janine's stupid bitch of a sister was staying with her for the weekend, and was in the kitchen calling the cops. Janine began hitting me and trying to claw my eyes, and I made a few punches in her direction, which were ENTIRELY IN SELF DEFENSE, but Barry, dumb shit that he is, only taped the part of me punching Janine in the face, and not what she did immediately before that to deserve it.

When the cops came, instead of running at the first sign of noise LIKE I TOLD HIM TO, Barry froze like a fucking deer in the headlights and that's how they found him, still crouched in the bushes, with the camera in his hand. Dumb ass. My supposed friend became the prosecution's best witness, and his video tape, which I had planned on putting up on the new SCUMSQUAT web site when it was finished, was taken as evidence and pretty much sealed my fate.

Issue #4, because of all the legal hassles, never went to press, but I have been releasing a VERY SMALL NUMBER of limited edition, signed and numbered photocopies, for the very reasonable price of $20, because of the instant notoriety and collectible status it received. Unfortunately, the video stills cannot be included, although I am working on getting a copy for my future website, which will document all the hypocrisy, bullshit, and total persecution I have been undergoing since this all began.

So, in eighteen months, with good behavior, I will be out. Not counting the appeal, of course, because the judge completely ignored some compelling evidence that Janine was not so terrified of me as she lyingly claimed in the court (which I cannot expose here because it will be a cornerstone of my appeal, but let's just say it involved plenty of offers for SEX during the time I was supposedly "harassing" her, which she later said was only to get me away from her because she was scared, but which I have PROOF is bullshit and which anyway doesn't make any sense when you think about it. I mean, trying to fuck me because you want to get AWAY from me? Right.) Anyway, naturally they take a woman's word over a man's every time, and none of this came out in the trial. But I'm not bitter, I will face my fate stoically and am already working on a zine I hope to produce from prison, which will document my time behind bars and hopefully prove that Janine Price is not the innocent little "victim" she claims to be but a truly screwed up, dangerous psycho that everybody in Denver can't stand and is afraid of and won't even deal with now.

Meanwhile, I need to give props and some serious shout-outs to my homeez who have been on my side through this whole thing. So listen up. First, thanks to Ned Trini, the editor of Twattle! zine, who interviewed me for Twattle! number 6 and who produced the amazing Brian Smelt Tribute Issue (available for two bucks from Ned at Box 16-34, Yakima, WA—check it out!!) Second, I have to give props to my mom, who has been totally understanding through this whole thing. There, mom, you happy now?

Also I need to say a big FUCK YOU to the following perps, twerps, and general scumbags: first, to Tory T., the prick behind FonDooDoo, that shitty, unoriginal zine from Syracuse, who completely ripped off my idea of doing record reviews with little icons (don't deny it you little fuck, that was MY IDEA)...and to Marcy Blum, of Shmagel Times in Cambridge, the cunt who claimed I stole her essay "Why Only Assholes Wear Ray-Bans" for my own essay "Why Only Assholes Wear Foster-Grants", which is TOTAL FUCKING BULLSHIT, and anyway, if you think your ideas are so precious that you're afraid of influencing other people's ideas then why are you putting out a zine in the first place, huh? Besides which your precious fucking essay SUCKED, sister. All I can say is, you're lucky you live in Massa Two-Shits, baby.

Finally, to all you assholes who have criticized SCUM-SQUAT and written me stupid letters claiming that I brought my problems on myself: FUCK YOU. I'm not crying, I'm not complaining, you've all wanted me to fail because you yourselves just SUCK so much that you can't take it.

As of February 2nd, please send checks, stamps, and cigarettes to Brian Smelt, #440119471 c/o Dept. of Corrections, Denver. I will be back, and you all better watch out!

Peace.

Brian Smelt
Editor, Publisher, Writer, Designer, and Creator
SCUMSQUAT Magazine (entire contents copyrighted and trademarked 2002 by Brian Smelt. All rights reserved.)

Nightmares

It's late, you're making tea, the night is quiet and still. The phone goes off and you grab it before the second ring, so as not to wake the person sleeping in the next room.

"Hello, Tim? It's me."

It's me. Which is worse: that after five years she still considers herself to be the only me in your life, or that you respond as if it were true?

"Oh, hi. How are you doing?"

"Not so good," she says. "Do you have a minute?"

What she tells you is sad, though hardly surprising. You knew something like this would probably happen, even if you hoped it wouldn't. In your more cynical moments you thought that the two of them together meant there were two less miserable people elsewhere in the world.

"He was cheating on me. It started after the baby was born. I began having my suspicions about six months ago, and then I hacked into his e-mail account and it was all right there. My lawyer had him served with divorce papers today. The person he's

113

sleeping with is engaged, and I found out who her fiancé is. I called him up and told him what was going on. We're having lunch tomorrow to talk about it."

You don't know what to say, you tell her.

"I wanted to tell you how sorry I am for the way things ended between us. If it's any comfort, just know that I've been paid back in spades, call it karma or whatever. I don't know if it means anything to you, but I wanted you to know that you were the best boyfriend I ever had, you treated me nicer and made me laugh more than anybody."

Thank you, you say.

"Remember those nights at Coney Island High and Green Door? Remember hanging out with Mike and Marlena and Flip, and Chris and Ally, and how much fun we used to have dancing and just being silly?"

You remember, you tell her.

"I felt like after you and I split, I never had any time to mourn our relationship."

That's because you were too busy playing Betty Crocker for some toolbox from Queens, you think. You can still hear her screaming how blue-collar men were more noble and decent. She listened to a lot of Springsteen back then.

"It felt like I was in a cult, he was just so domineering and controlling. I thought I wanted that at the time, a real strong person, a father figure, to tell me what to do, what to wear, how to think."

You get chills. You can still see him in his wife beater, wallet chain hanging off his work pants, beefy arms crossed as he leans against the car outside, looking around himself with an air of smug triumph. And you, standing in the spare room that was your own self-imposed exile, peeking cowardly from behind the curtain, watching as she runs outside in her tightest cutoffs and

114

her hair done in a way you'd never seen before, careful not to kiss him until they're inside the car.

"That's the last time I'll ever go out with somebody with tattoos," she says. "What did you used to call him?"

"A rockabully."

"Yeah, that's it. It still makes me laugh. Well, if it's any consolation you were completely right about him, everything you said about him was true. You had him pegged as a phony from the beginning. Boy, was I dumb. You always accepted and loved me for who I was, and I'm just realizing how special that was."

"Thank you."

"Can I ask you something? I know you're married now, and I really hope you're happy, but...are you guys going to stay together?"

Ah. Ah ah.

You remember the last time you spoke with her. It was a year after she'd left, and you had a terrible nightmare that she was in grave danger. You saw her screaming, trapped, being pulled down into a dark cave that was filled, hilariously, with translucent sticky goo. You remember in your dream she screamed for you to help her as you flew above the scene, and that you looked down and called, "I can't help you, I'm sorry," and then flew away. It was such a creepy dream that you couldn't shake the feeling that something was terribly wrong, and the next day you finally broke down and left her a voicemail. When she called you back the following night, she told you that you had left the message exactly in the middle of her wedding ceremony.

You decide to aerosolize.

"Well," you say, "I certainly hope so. But the truth is, Gwen, none of us has a crystal ball, we can't see into the future. We just take things one day at a time and do our best, and that's about all anybody can do."

115

She agrees and her voice is dreamy and distant, like it's the most profound thing she's ever heard. She tells you she's on tranquilizers.

"I wish you the very best, and happiness," she says. "Maybe we could get together for dinner sometime."

Maybe, you tell her. You thank her for calling.

You put down the phone and your hand is trembling, it's like the saddest song Yo La Tengo ever sang. You go quietly into the other room where your wife, your beautiful bride, is sleeping, surrounded by the cats. You smooth her hair, kiss her forehead and chew your lip as you go back to the living room to finish packing. You're leaving her.

The Cough

I've been sick for a year. That might come as a surprise to my friends, most of whom would probably say it's been much longer than that, but I mean really, physically ill. It's been a full year, with only scattered reprieves, of colds, flu, chills, aches, sore throats, coughs and insomnia.

Not that it really surprises me. It was a bad year. I started 2001 with a painful separation from my wife, then endured the depredations and prevarications of a vindictive, unstable family member. I spent much of the year homeless, out of work and going deeper into debt. I found myself in new, unfamiliar neighborhoods far from the quiet, close-knit Williamsburg community I had called home for nearly a decade. I had a bicycle, a backpack and a cell phone, and not much else. I was edgy, depressed, manic. I don't think I put more than two continuous hours of sleep together for the entire year. Of course I was sick.

I tried to stay healthy, I really did. I quit drinking, cut down the smoking and committed myself to a more active regimen. I rode my bicycle everywhere I could, and bought myself one of those little abdomen wheel things. Every morning, wherever I was staying, I would make myself do three sets of 10 rolls, like a little ball of pizza dough trying to roll itself flat. I felt it was starting to help, but then I got a freak muscle spasm in my neck and was bedridden for two weeks, barely able to get myself up to go to the bathroom. Each attempt was a comical, 10-minute modern dance involving a complex weight-balancing and shifting process that invariably left me screaming in agony. August was the worst month, when every ailment came on all at once and I was a spasming, flu-riddled mess. I vowed to get myself to a doctor right after Labor Day. And then all hell broke loose.

Watching the planes fly into the World Trade Center my first thought was "Oh, now terrorists are blowing up the world. Sure, why not?" That's not to minimize the sickness or horror I felt, but because it was the ultimate just-when-you-think-things-can't-get-any-worse moment, an absurd cosmic one-upmanship that pushed my already teetering psyche right to the edge.

When I got back to Brooklyn that afternoon I wandered down Montague Street. The acrid air was thick brown, filled with soot and ash. It looked like nuclear winter. Common sense told me I should be walking away from the source and not toward it, but I couldn't help myself. I put my t-shirt over my face and went down to the promenade, where masses of people were milling around. I sat down on a bench and stared. And cried. I went back to the promenade later that evening, and again late that night, then early the next morning. I began making four or five trips every day, sitting for hours at a time. I attended a few candlelight vigils, walked and talked for hours with friends by the distant glow of the klieg lights.

The cough started on the fourth or fifth day. At the time I

shrugged it off, because I had been sick in one form or another for nine months, but while sitting with friends at a coffee shop on Montague St. I jokingly said that I had "World Trade Syndrome." But I never really thought it would turn out I was right.

It became something of a joke at work; the guy in the next cubicle was constantly offering me cough medicine, Dayquil, drops, lozenges, anything to get me to shut up. It was a dry, deep, hacking cough, relentless and strong. My coworkers had often complained about the poor air quality in the office, so I bought an air filter and humidifier for my cubicle. This seemed to help, so I got another for home. My cough subsided, but it never completely went away. Meanwhile, my other illnesses proceeded apace: I got sick, I got better, I got sick, I got better.

I didn't go to my doctor for a long time. When I finally did, the first thing she asked was, "Why didn't you come and see me sooner?" I shrugged. "Because I felt too lousy," was my answer. She laughed, but I think she understood, too.

The doctor told me I had The Cough. I don't recall the medical term she used, but she said my lungs had become over sensitized to irritants, due to my exposure to the toxins and chemicals in the air after 9/11. Although she didn't think I had asthma, that it was probably only bronchial spasms, it was still too early to tell. The doctor prescribed an inhaler, which I am still using, and it has helped a great deal. I probably don't cough more than 10 times an hour now, and they're much milder. I have to go back for a follow-up visit soon. I keep trying to tell myself I can put it off, but I know I shouldn't.

On New Year's Eve, a few minutes before midnight, I raised a glass with a good friend. We reflected on what a hard year 2001 had been. I talked about my health problems. "I feel like I spent the whole last year just trying to get well," I told him. My friend thought for a minute, then answered, "If that's the case, then why don't you make this year all about *staying* well?" It was so simple; my friend was right. A few days later I flipped through my healthcare provider directory, and started looking under "psychologists."

Webels

Kirby says that Boo-T-Rex is fat, but I'm not so sure. It's hard to tell by the picture, and according to the ad she's five-ten and weighs 150, which isn't bad. Boo's ad says she has an ass like a 'Christmas ham' from all the kickboxing she does, and that she looks like John Singer Sargent's "Madame X." Looking at the picture I figure it's a stretch, but possible. I ask Boo if she wants to go to the park and toss around a Frisbee. She agrees and we decide to meet at a nearby cafe.

In the movie version of my life, you would see me sitting at the cafe table, reading the menu, waiting for Boo-T-Rex. I look down and see the still surface of my coffee broken by a ripple. A few seconds later, another ripple. Then another, and another, gaining in speed and severity as a faint booming sound grows louder. A shadow blocks out the sun and engulfs me, as I look up in horror and...and...

Boo-T-Rex descends onto the chair. The poor chair. I act

nonchalant, I'm friendly and polite. We exchange small talk, order some food, then I grab my cell phone.

"Would you excuse me please? I need to make a call."

I get outside and dial. This is all Kirby's fault, he got me into this. Last year he put an ad online and said he got so much pussy that it nearly made him gay. He's home.

"Kirby! You gotta help me!"

"Dude, I told you she was fat."

"But not like this! A little pudgy, sure, but you have no idea, you can't believe it! Total disconnect from reality here. 150 pounds? I think she meant 150 kilos, bro."

"Oh no."

"You know that line about having an ass like a Christmas ham? Dude, she's got the whole pig back there! Stop laughing, damn you! What do I do?"

"I'm sorry, man. Look, just relax. I'll call you back in ten minutes. Make it seem like some emergency. Just tell her something's come up, and you have to split. Then you come over and watch a movie."

"I can't do that, it's way too obvious."

"I just got *Star 80* on DVD."

"I'll be there in an hour."

SaucyTart212 is going to be at a bar in the East Village, at a friend's birthday party. It's as good a place to meet as any. She's been emailing me for a few days, sending me lots of pictures. She's cute, and seems eager to meet me. I go to the Russian Baths after work to unwind, and at the appointed time I head to the bar.

Saucy is easy to spot, she's the only one in a red dress. She looks good, like in the pictures, except that she looks a bit heavier in person. Not Boo-T-Rex heavy, but still. She's sitting with a big group, so I wave and she comes over.

We get a small table away from the crowd. Almost immediately I know something's wrong. Saucy is distracted, distant. Every attempt at conversation fizzles. I try to figure it out. I don't think it's my looks, because the picture in my ad is recent. I don't know what it is. It hardly matters, I just know I want to leave. It's been five minutes. I go to the bar and get some drinks.

Saucy's phone keeps ringing, and when it's not ringing she fiddles with it anyway. People come over to talk to her, but she doesn't introduce me. Then somebody plays a Johnny Cash song on the jukebox and she perks up. "I love Johnny Cash," she says. "When I was in L.A., there was this bar I'd go to. Whenever they played 'Ring of Fire' the bartender would pour booze into this thing and light it, and there would be a ring of fire around the bar. It was really cool."

Saucy tells me that the people at the party are all people she met online, through one of those journal-writing sites. I ask her which one, but Saucy won't tell. She shakes her head gravely, as if she were hiding dead bodies and weapons-grade plutonium, instead of the usual insipid posts about the crush she has on some tattooed Scorpio girl. It's a world I don't understand, these people who build their entire identities and personalities online, who imagine themselves as leading wild and dangerous lives when in reality they're just consumers of kookiness. Saucy is a web rebel. A *webel*.

A few more of Saucy's online friends show up. They're drunk and arguing loudly about 80s metal bands. Saucy is delighted. "These guys are just so funny, I could listen to them all night!" I don't say anything.

There's talk of going to a karaoke bar. Saucy tells me that

she's going to be "very social" all night, so that I shouldn't count too much on her attention or conversation. I tell her it's all right, because I'm going home anyway. I grab my coat and head for the door. It's just as well. I never liked Johnny Cash, I always thought he was full of shit. Just like SaucyTart212.

There are other dates. Not all of them start badly, but they always wind up that way. I have a good date with SumpnSpecial, then she disappears without even a thank you. VanGoGoGirl, a painter, takes me to a museum, and afterwards we plan another date. The day we're supposed to meet she doesn't call. I leave her a message, send an email, but there's no response. It's depressing.

A co-worker tells me not to worry, that when she did online dating sometimes she would have a good time with someone and just never contact him again, for no particular reason. "Don't take it personally," she says. Okay, I tell her, but I know: I'm going to take it personally.

I'm picking up FunkyButChic when she gets off work. I get to the place a few minutes early, to check her out surreptitiously. If she looks like trouble, or is big as a house, or has only one eye, I'm leaving. Funky works at a beauty products store. The store has big windows facing the street, so I walk by slowly, looking for her. Everybody in the store is wearing white lab coats. On my second pass I spot Funky, behind the counter. Her picture was pretty good, but in person she's beautiful. She's got red hair and cute glasses. She looks very sexy in her white lab coat, like a Bond girl. I go into the store and loiter near the skin creams. Funky is talking with a customer, but she sees me and smiles. It's a beautiful smile. I motion that I'll be waiting outside. She nods and holds up five fingers.

A little while later Funky emerges. The lab coat's gone and I can see that she's got a good body and is well dressed, with high boots and a tight cashmere sweater and sexy skirt. It's going to be a good night, I can feel it. My cell phone rings. I hesitate.

"Do you need to get that?" Funky asks. "It's okay, I totally understand." Funky is smiling at me, her head slightly tilted. I look at the screen on the phone. It's Kirby. I put the phone back in my bag.

"No," I say, as we start walking in no particular direction, "It's nobody I need to talk to right now."

Plus-Size

1.

When the woman from the agency called I was living on a friend's futon and my prospects were grim. My marriage had recently broken up and the company I was working for had folded a few weeks later. For some reason I wasn't eligible for unemployment, I don't remember why. I tried to find work but the economy was bad that summer and nobody was hiring. Even some of the temp agencies were shutting down. I had a little money saved but that was going fast.

To keep myself sane I would ride my bike around Prospect Park. I would go around and around, sometimes for hours. At night I did my best to stay out of my friend's way. It wasn't hard. Kirby met women online and was always going on dates. He brought a lot of them home. I would pretend to be asleep when they came in, and lie awake listening to the sounds coming from the other room. When the women tiptoed out in the morning, disheveled and carrying their shoes, I would watch them through the slits of my eyes from the futon and rate them. There were a few clunkers, but most of them were very good looking. I would fantasize about having sex with all of them, and then jerk off after Kirby left for work. One of them even took pity on me, a cute little English music promoter who stayed with us for a week while she scouted local bands. She fucked Kirby at night and me during the day. Then she went back to England and I went back to the futon.

I was getting ready for my bike ride one morning when the phone rang. A woman's voice asked for me and I said speaking. She told me there was an opening for an image cropper at a midtown fashion company, temp to perm, if I was interested. I said that yes, it sounded very interesting, and tried to stay calm as I took down the information. I had fifty dollars in the bank. I wouldn't have cared if they turned depleted uranium into baby formula.

2.

According to the company website, Chunky But Funky Fashions is "the leading catalog of cutting edge, plus-size fashions for the large and in charge woman." There were also divisions for men (Bruno), children (Big Kids!), and even something called *Gran Mujer,* for the heavyset Latina woman. In this great land of opportunity of ours, everybody could be fat. I learned that plus-size clothing was the fastest-growing part of the fashion market, and there is no other way I can put that without it sounding funny. That's why they needed the extra help.

My job was to pull the images from the catalogs and then fit them into the templates for the website. It was easy enough but there were a lot of images to do and always more coming in.

I worked with two guys, Tommy the Yank and Slo-mo. They called him Tommy the Yank because when a computer had a problem he would shut it down by yanking the power cord out of the wall. He had fried a few hard drives that way before somebody set him straight, but the name had stuck.

Tommy was a ladies' man. For a company that catered mostly to old fatties, Chunky But Funky had a lot of beautiful young women working there. Tommy knew them all. When he wasn't cropping images or yanking cords he was hanging around one of their cubicles, making small talk. Tommy was 30 and balding and still lived with his parents, but I heard he had managed to screw of few of them. Everybody loved Tommy.

Slo-mo said he got his nickname because of his slow southern drawl, but I wasn't so sure. He had been a security guard at Chunky But Funky for 10 years before becoming an image cropper. It showed. He had the same aloof, slightly superior attitude of anybody who has spent a prolonged time wearing a polyester uniform with a shield-shaped patch sewn on one sleeve.

Slo-mo had a radio and he liked to play it. That wasn't a problem, but Slo-mo kept it on the same lite R&B station. He never changed it. Sometimes they would play something good—Spinners, Aretha, Lionel Richie—but for every good song that came on they'd play hours of inane urban dreck: wailing, sobbing ballads or suggestive softcore rapping about booties and parties and getting things started. Of course, they also played Whitney Houston in constant rotation, and Whitney has got to be the most overrated singer since Streisand. All that gargling and warbling; it was horrible. Give me Celine Dion any day. I don't' care what anybody says, Celine has soul. Whitney Houston is just a screeching drug addict, about as emotionally connected and convincing as any second-rate porn actress.

People would ask Slo-mo to turn it down and he would give that superior little security guard sneer and ignore them. When it got to be too much I'd put my headphones on, but every time I wanted to tell him to shut it off I'd remember Kirby's futon, and it didn't seem so bad after all.

3.

After a few weeks they hired me on full-time. With a steady paycheck I was able get a small apartment on the edge of a bad neighborhood. At night I would listen to the popping of distant gunshots and drift into a deep sleep, imagining they were fireworks being shot off in my honor. Sometimes the shots would be closer, and when I'd leave for work in the morning there would be the familiar yellow crime scene tape, and a cop placing numbered cones next to the empty shells. Gang members stood guard outside the drug deli down the block, looking evil and innocent. I would pass them on my way to work and they would still be there when I got home at night. They never bothered me. I didn't know if they thought I was a cop or if they figured that any white boy crazy enough to live in that neighborhood must have bigger problems than they had. I never asked.

4.

One day Slo-mo disappeared. He left at the end of his shift and never came back. Two weeks went by, then three. After a month we got the news: Slo-mo had moved to Atlanta, and was working at a Kinko's. It was weird. I rummaged through my desk and found a letter opener in the drawer. Then I walked over to where Tommy the Yank sat.

"Follow me," I said.

We went to Slo-mo's cubicle. I pointed to the radio and looked at Tommy.

"Go ahead, man, do your stuff."

Tommy didn't need to be asked twice. He reached around and grabbed the cord and yanked it from the wall. Then I turned the radio face up and stabbed the fucking thing full of holes with the letter opener. I cut the power cord and tied the whole thing up and hung it in front of Slo-mo's computer. One of the designers walked by and saw what we were doing.

"Praise be to God," she said.

The radio stayed up there for a few days, then it was gone. I didn't know what happened to it and I didn't care. Fuck it and him and Whitney Houston too.

5.

Tommy the Yank was next.

Tommy didn't disappear like Slo-mo; he found a new job and gave his two weeks. I wasn't surprised. For a few months I could see that Tommy was unhappy. It seemed to happen overnight. He had retreated into himself; instead of organizing drinks or hitting on women he stayed in his cubicle, surfing the web and hardly talking to anybody. I asked him what was wrong, or if there was anything I could do, and he gave me a strange sort of smile.

"You don't understand," he said. "I used to care, I used to like working here. But nothing ever changes. They..." Tommy's voice trailed off, and he made a vague spinning gesture with his hand. "Never mind," he started again, "it's nothing. Forget I said anything."

On his last day we all went out for drinks. About a dozen of us showed up, including Gerri. Gerri was the most beautiful woman at Chunky But Funky, a wild-eyed and slightly crazy blonde from editorial. Every guy in the company wanted her, a situation that was made even more volatile by the stories flying around that she would put out for the right guy. On the rare occasions when I had some business on her floor, I would see at least two guys hovering around her cubicle, cracking jokes and jockeying for position like teenagers. The rumor in the office was that she and Tommy had something going, but they both denied it.

Gerri could put away the wine. At some point we began to talk. Gerri told me about her life. She seemed to have lived a fairly aimless existence of some privilege. There was a rich daddy in Oregon and plenty of prep schools and summers in Europe. She had dropped out of college a week before graduation to run away with a Spaniard. It had cost daddy a fortune. I couldn't relate except for the aimless existence part, but I got the feeling Gerri was interested in me because I was the only man at Chunky But Funky who had never shown any interest in her.

We talked for a long time. Gerri drank her wine, and I spaced my drinks carefully, with plenty of water between each one. I never liked getting drunk around co-workers; it only caused hard feelings and complications later on. Finally it was late and I was tired. There were only a handful of people from work left at the bar, and I was the only one who wasn't drunk. I got my coat and went over to say good night.

"Where are you going?" Gerri asked.

"Home. It's getting late."

Gerri grabbed my arm and her eyes flashed.

"Don't go! You can't leave yet!"

It happened so fast I didn't have time to react. Gerri was still gripping my arm, and her other hand came around and grabbed the back of my head and pulled it towards her. I could smell the wine as her tongue jabbed at my face. She hit my chin, an eye, and both nostrils, then she came in close and snaked the wet and slimy thing into my ear canal.

"Come into the bathroom with me," she slurred. "I want to show you something."

I tried to get away, but she was strong. Her tongue came at me again, and this time it hit the target and began fishing and flopping inside my mouth. Even drunk, she could do some amazing tricks with that tongue. She probably used it to tie her shoelaces.

I pushed her away again and she licked my other eye.

"What's wrong?" she gasped.

"What about Tommy?"

"Fuck Tommy!" she screamed. "He's leaving. Besides, he's too skinny for me. You're built like a real man; you've got some meat on your bones. You've got an ass I can actually grab! Come on, let's go in the bathroom, it won't take long." Then she grabbed my ass with both hands and squeezed so hard that I yelped. I looked over at Tommy. He looked stricken. He and a few of the other guys were watching with heavy, drunken eyes.

It was the desperate voyeurism, the morning-after office gossip humiliation, the whole lonely middle-aged cocktail lounge tragedy of it all that I hated. It was like a scene from a Cassavetes movie. I suddenly felt very sad.

I pulled Gerri's arms from around my neck and held them down.

"No," I said. I let her go and raised a little salute to the guys. Then I walked out.

A few weeks earlier I might have done it. But I had recently met someone. Her name was Dolly. She was tall and slim and had the biggest, roundest blue eyes I had ever seen. She fed me steak and wine and told me I was beautiful. She read my stories and laughed at all the right parts. She had a good job, loved her family, and wasn't a frustrated anything. By Manhattan standards she was something of a miracle.

Dolly had an apartment in Chelsea. It was nice being out of the ghetto for a change. I got to the building and she buzzed me in.

"How was it?" she asked.

"I've just been tongue raped."

"My poor baby," she said.

6.

When my lease was up I moved out of the ghetto and in with Dolly. It was a small place but we were happy. One morning as I was getting ready for work I pulled my jeans on. I looked at Dolly.

"Did you wash these jeans recently?"

"Nope."

"They seem tight."

"You're putting on weight, sweet pea."

"Am I? I guess you're right." I took them off and tried on another pair.

"Damn, these other pants are getting snug too! You know what this means, don't you baby?"

"What?"

"I'm becoming one of them!"

"One of what?"

"I'm turning plus-size, baby, I'm CHUNKY BUT FUNKY!"

Pretty soon I wasn't laughing about it. I couldn't fit into any of my pants any more, and had to buy one size bigger. Then they started getting snug, and I had to go up another size. I went up 4 sizes in six months. I wasn't fat, but I had a belly now, for the first time in my life. Being homeless and unemployed might have made me depressed and crazy, but it also kept me thin. I wanted to look good for Dolly so I joined a gym and started exercising and watching what I ate. Dolly said she didn't mind the extra pounds because it only meant that I was happy. She was right. And this time I hoped that my happiness, unlike my 32-inch waist, would last.

Literary Anarchists Mobilizing Everywhere!

"Revolution!"

That's what the advertisement said, running down the left-hand column of the online magazine I was reading. "Help us take back literature from the over-educated elites and rich fops! Join the revolution that will bring back meaning and relevance to American letters!"

Now, it just so happens that there are few things in life I enjoy more than a good revolution—especially the rhetorical kind—so I clicked on the link. And that's how I became involved with Literary Anarchists Mobilizing Everywhere!, or L.A.M.E!

I had just published my first novel, *The Cheese-Thunderer's God*, under my own Boethius Press imprint. If you've ever peddled a self-published novel then you know why I was feeling about as popular as a weenie salesman at the Wailing Wall. I was looking for ways to boost my profile. Being part of a group of literary outlaws—even self-proclaimed outlaws—couldn't hurt. If I was a little unnerved by the claims on the L.A.M.E!

website that their goal was nothing less than "toppling the twin towers of modern literature and big publishing," I suppressed my anxiety. A little controversy, I told myself over and over, never hurt.

I sent the group an email, telling them about myself and why I was a good candidate. The first part was easy enough—I'd had a long and somewhat colorful career in the alternative press—but the second part was more difficult. I tried to imagine what a literary revolution might look like, and what part I might play in one, but the only image I could conjure involved face paint, machetes, and a Graham Greene novel or two. I don't remember exactly what I wrote, but it did the trick. A few days later I got a response from Peter "Prince" Mishkin, co-founder of the group:

> *Thank you for your interest in Literary Anarchists Mobilizing Everywhere! Before we can make a final decision on your application, we need one more piece of information: what is your name going to be?*

I wrote back, in somewhat confused haste, *Umm...Dan Greenbaum, same as always?*

My fingers hadn't left the mouse before Prince's reply dingdonged in my inbox.

> *Not your real name. . .your Underground name!*

I suppose I should have done it before, but it wasn't until this point that I really explored the Literary Anarchists Mobilizing Everywhere website! I mean, *Everywhere!* website. As I scanned the list of L.A.M.E! writers I understood what Prince was asking: all the members (approximately three dozen by my estimate), had adopted some kind of "handle," or nickname, to signal both their solidarity with the cause as well as to differentiate themselves, according to the site, from the "mindless, lock-step, groupthink hordes" of the "literary-industrial complex."

Besides Peter "Prince" Mishkin the other co-founders were named "Jolly" Jack Crapper and Stan "Squared" Stanislawski. Other members went by handles like Betty Bomb, Nuclear Neal, and Kooky Ken; still others opted for more generic descriptions, such as The Jackal or, oddly enough, Car Door. There were a few members who combined computer lingo and spellings (DV80r and 71b3r80r, for example), as well as a heavy metal fanzine writer who simply went by the symbol \m/.

Most of them published zines—that is to say, collections of random thoughts assembled at irregular intervals and usually photocopied and stapled at a local copy shop—with names like *Snot Puppy*, *Hell Bastard on Crack*, and the ever-enigmatic and eponymous *Car Door.*

My dinging inbox interrupted my revolutionary studies. It was another email from Prince Mishkin; it seemed to address the confusion I was feeling.

You cannot be a true Undergrounder unless you have an Underground Name. It's the L.A.M.E! way!

Having always been of the mindset that personas worked better in fiction than in reality, I had no idea what to say. I suggested the first thing I could think of. *How about 'Dan The Man'?* I wrote.

Can't. It's taken. It's being used by Stan "The Man" Stanislawski.

I re-checked the L.A.M.E! website and wrote back to Prince a minute later: this Stanislawski person was listed as Stan "Squared." What gave?

"Squared" is for internal L.A.M.E! use only. Stan "The Man" is what he uses for business and formal occasions.

Well, that settled it. Or did it? How many other members, I wondered, had spare monikers just lying around? How many were hogging up good names that they only trotted out on special occasions? Was that fair? I thought I might write a formal letter of complaint. Meanwhile, I dedicated myself to coming up with a L.A.M.E! name.

My first choice was "Dirty" Danny Greenbaum, but "Dirty Danny" was the name of a cartoon character, and cartoonists are notoriously litigious, so after a long list of discarded attempts that included "Dangerous" Dan, Danosaurus Rex, and Dan1m80r, I finally settled on Danny "Ducats" Greenbaum—a wry play on my Jewish heritage as well as what I hoped would be a self-fulfilling prophecy. I sent my choice to Prince Mishkin and waited apprehensively for his approval. Once again, his reply was not long in coming:

Congratulations, Danny Ducats! Welcome to L.A.M.E!

L.A.M.E! life centered almost exclusively around the website. As far as websites went it was one of the worst I'd ever seen: fonts of all different sizes and shapes, lots of text that was bold and ALL CAPS and red or blue, all of it talking about the Revolution, the conspiracy of Big Publishing to keep down the "real" writers in the country, the writers they were afraid of because they told the TRUTH, the ugly truth that nobody wanted to hear! It was too dangerous! That was why L.A.M.E! had been founded, to blow the whistle on it all, to sink the whole decadent *Titanic* of American Literature! The Revolution was coming! The L.A.M.E! Revolution!!!

But what did this revolution actually consist of? What steps would be taken, and what would replace that which was torn down? I clicked through the site, looking for answers. Eventually I settled on Prince Mishkin's daily journal, called "Destroying The Dandies," where he posted regular updates on the progress of the revolution—which, best as I could tell, consisted mainly of attacking the same two or three authors. In fact, as I soon learned, Mishkin had founded L.A.M.E! in order to protest the work of one writer in particular: Jerome Soforth Wiggins.

Jerome Soforth Wiggins! No other man, no matter how evil or vile—mass murderer, insane dictator, or child molester—could move Prince Mishkin to such crescendos of angry ululation, the fugue state of verbal violence that he displayed day after day on "Destroying The Dandies." Wiggins was a fraud, a cheat, and the "poster boy of corruption" in the literary world. He was born rich, raised well, educated in the best schools—and therefore, according to Mishkin, ineligible to participate in the world of letters. Literature, said Mishkin, was the sole rightful province of the lower classes, the farmers and working folk whose copies of Thackeray and Dickens and Shakespeare had been pried from the hands of their wailing, sobbing children by corrupt capitalists sometime around 1900. And nobody embodied these wax-mustachioed, top-hatted villains more than that wealthy banker's son, Jerome Soforth Wiggins, whose great crime against humanity was that he had once applied for—and received—a writing grant that he clearly did not need!

Piggish? Certainly. But to Mishkin that made Wiggins a literary Hitler, the lifelong enemy of real writers everywhere, and deserving of a long and painful professional death.

Day in and day out, Mishkin's attacks continued against Wiggins: Fraud! Charlatan! Silk-diapered dandy! Silver-spooned sophisticate! And I, for a few months at least, was right there with Mishkin, cheering him. A lot of modern authors deserved to be knocked off their high perch, especially those of the "ironic" or "postmodern" schools, those callow souls who hid their cynicism behind mockery and insincerity. If Mishkin wanted to knock them down a few pegs, it was fine by me.

I submitted my picture and a short bio to the Webmaster, and a few days later he added me to the L.A.M.E! website. Right away I received a number of congratulatory emails. If I still felt silly about being Danny "Ducats" Greenbaum (and I did), then it lessened somewhat in the wave of genuine warmth and camaraderie with which I was greeted. A few people bought copies of my book, and some even took the time to write encouraging reviews for their zines and websites. As I clicked around the L.A.M.E! website I felt, for the first time, a sense of belonging to something worthwhile. And me, a published novelist, no less! Even if the company that published the novel was my own, making it somewhat less impressive, I soon realized with some satisfaction that I was the only L.A.M.E! member with a published novel at all.

It was a fact that, oddly enough, became the basis for my next point of friction with the L.A.M.E! leadership.

Dear Prince Mishkin,

I've been kicking around the site for a few weeks now. I hope this isn't a stupid question but I have to ask: do any of the other L.A.M.E! members actually, you know, write anything?

Thanks, Danny "Ducats"

This time the answer didn't arrive immediately. It was a few days before I got his reply:

Danny, the purpose of Literary Anarchists Mobilizing Everywhere! is to awaken complacent readers, attack the mindless and disconnected hacks posing as authors, and completely tear down the corrupt edifice of publishing! We need to give literature back to real people, to the working classes where it belongs!

Prince Mishkin

Hi Prince—

Okay, I hear you...sort of. I guess my question is, awaken readers to what? What's the point if we're not actually offering any alternative, in terms of writing? Also, not to put too fine a point on it, but wouldn't tearing down the existing publishing model also hurt a lot of working people? What about the printers, truck drivers, hi-lo operators and the rest? Is the idea that if they're out of work they'll have more time to read? Just wondering.

Regards, Danny

Another few days passed before the answer came:

DON'T GET HUNG UP ON SPECIFICS! OUR GOAL MUST BE FIRST AND FOREMOST TO GET ATTENTION FOR OUR CAUSE! WE CAN WORRY ABOUT BOOKS LATER! ALL OF OUR WRITERS ARE TRUE UNDERGROUND ZINESTERS AND HELL-RAISERS! THEY'RE TOO AUTHENTIC FOR THE EFFETE LIBERALS IN THE NEW YORK

*PUBLISHING HOUSES! YOU SOUND LIKE YOU
MIGHT BE PRETTY BRAINWASHED, I SEE YOU
MADE THE COVER OF YOUR BOOK LOOK
REAL PRETTY. WAKE UP AND SMELL THE
REVOLUTION!*

MY RIGHT EYE — I mean, my right eye twitched. There
was that word again: *authentic.* I had always considered authenticity to be something that came from within, and was based on a
complex interrelationship of psychology, intellect, and ethics, for
starters. It was a goal one strived for, not an end unto itself, and
certainly not a marketing tool. The more I explored the
L.A.M.E! website the more I realized that, in Mishkin's hands,
"authenticity" really described an esthetics of amateurism: a
world that favored typewriters over computers, tape over glue,
photocopy over offset. And if you rejected the Industrial Revolution altogether and scratched the words out with a stone tool or
the point of a charred stick, then so much the better! One was
expected not to refine, edit, or exhibit any literary finesse what-
soever. Whether the writing was any good was not the point;
doubters could always be chased away with the accusation that
they were not "authentic."

As I looked over the blurry cover icons for the various zines
offered by L.A.M.E! members, many of which were scrawled
with crayons and markers, I realized with a pang that *The
Cheese-Thunderer's God* looked hopelessly competent by
comparison.

I had a lot to learn about revolutions.

*The Future of Literature—so began one of Prince Mish-
kin's bromides around that time—belongs not in the
hands of the dainty professors and school-marm editors*

142

*of slick monthlies. It belongs to the real writers, writing
from the streets, who are living real lives of real struggle!*

*It is not the twee, self-involved navel-gazing of a Jerome
Soforth Wiggins that connects with the average reader,
but the kick-ass raw meat style of a Leo "The Lion" Brutus, or a Joe Typer!*

Here again, I felt a twinge—Wiggins, however glaring his literary flaws, had a long publishing career and several bestselling
novels to his credit—deflating somewhat Mishkin's claim that
Wiggins was incapable of connecting with average readers. I
could not have been the only person who noticed this, and I
assume somebody called him on it; the next day, without ad-
dressing his error directly, Mishkin's post tried to deflect such
criticism:

> *The brainwashed writer believes that "writers write." The
> brainwashed writer believes that selling a lot of books
> means a writer has "connected" with readers. Wrong!
> These are the pretty fantasies that have been fed to them
> by Big Publishing, and their cronies in the media world!*

I decided to turn my attention to more positive pursuits;
namely, to investigate those L.A.M.E! writers who Mishkin had
held up as shining examples of great Literature *vis-à-vis* Wiggins:
Leo "The Lion" Brutus and "Joe Typer."

Of all the emotions that welled up inside me as I first read
Joe Typer's stories, it's hard to say which was strongest: pity, re-
vulsion, or outright horror. He was an older man, living in a
Southern backwater and playing the *art brut* card to the hilt. He
had written 250 novels, none published, because (according to
Mishkin) the American people were not ready for his writing. I

navigated to Typer's website and found his latest "novel," the likes of which he was cranking out at a rate of 12 or 15 per year. The chapters were arranged by date, so I clicked one at random and began to read:

> *December 6: Engine light came on in the car. Took it to the garage. Had it checked. Nothing major.*
>
> *December 7: No mail today. Sunny. Might go for a walk. Had a sandwich for lunch.*

On and on it went like that, for 300 pages. And beyond that, 249 more "novels" just like it! 75,000 pages of engine lights and sandwiches! And interspersed with the details of his life, the chronicles of vehicular drama and trips to the supermarket, were constant boasts of how he, Joe Typer, was AMERICA'S GREATEST UNDERGROUND WRITER, better than Bukowski!

Typer was right about one thing: America was definitely not ready for his writing. If someday scientists discovered a planet that was populated entirely by public accountants and model train aficionados, I bet he'd sell like hotcakes.

This was the guy Mishkin pegged as the savior of literature? This was the guy American Publishing was too terrified to publish? This was the man I was supposed to throw a flowerpot through a window of *The New Yorker* on behalf of? Engine lights? I didn't even own a damn car.

I turned away from Mr. 0-for-250, Mr. Better Than Bukowski, and with a little more digging, came across the even sadder case of Leo "The Lion" Brutus. I say sadder because whereas at least Typer was out there doing his finger exercises every day, Brutus had written a novel 35 years ago and done nothing since. He had sent a copy to Bill Burroughs, who had written a polite and encouraging note back. That was it! That was his achievement. And it was a western! A bad one! A western filled with characters named Jeb and Clem who spoke like, "Now lissen here, li'l lady, a man's gotta do what a man's gotta do" and rode horses...named Hoss! They fought Injuns and made love to squaws! For 35 years! He hadn't written anything since! Did he have writer's block? Had he quit? What did it matter? I figured if Brutus ever wanted more novels he could always ask Joe Typer for a few. He'd never miss them.

I closed down my browser and put the computer to sleep. My normally sunny mood was dark. Is this what I was fighting for? Was this the Revolution? Was this what they meant by "underground," "reality," and "authenticity"?

I wasn't sure what to do. Quit? I remembered how good it felt when I first joined, the sense of belonging, of having a purpose. There were some nice people involved, people I wanted to get to know better. *Give me a sign,* I thought. *Maybe there's still a chance for me to do something positive.*

A week later I had my answer.

It was a strange-looking package, heavily taped and bearing foreign stamps, in a language and alphabet I did not recognize. It had been sent weeks earlier, according to the date on the cancellation stamp. I looked at the return address and discovered it had come from a remote part of Southeast Asia.

It took some doing but I finally got the package opened. It was from Stan "Squared" Stanislawski, who edited a literary zine called *The Mucus Times.* There were several issues enclosed. Stan lived in a small village and rode his bicycle miles through the jungle to the nearest cyber-café in order to put each issue together. *The Mucus Times* mostly featured the work of other L.A.M.E! members. Figuring it would only hasten my impending resignation, I took the package to the couch and began to

145

read. Only several hours later, as I reluctantly closed the back cover of the last issue, did I get up again. It was brilliant! A little uneven, to be sure, but the best stories had a lot of originality, style, courage-so this was where all the good writing had been hiding! Suddenly it came to me, the idea I was looking for.

I emailed the editor, thanking him for the package. I also mentioned, casually, that if he were ever interested in doing a book, then I would be very interested in publishing it.

A few weeks later I got the manuscript. It was the best writing from *The Mucus Times* and chronicled the activism of L.A.M.E! against the literary establishment, including a number of Prince Mishkin's screeds against Jerome Soforth Wiggins. There were selections from Joe Typer and Leo "The Lion" as well, but in the context of the collection even they didn't seem too bad.

I knew that I had to publish the book. It would put L.A.M.E! on the map, and launch Boethius Press into the small publishing legend books!

I spent the next few weeks reading, polishing, and formatting the manuscript. I hired a famous illustrator to do the cover, at only a fraction of his usual rate. I hustled meetings and business contacts like crazy. I wrote to Stan and Prince: the book was going to be huge! Several national distributors were interested! We might need a conservative first printing of 5,000 or more! Looking into securing bank loans and lines of credit! The revolution will be a success!

The next time I went to the L.A.M.E! website, at first I thought I had gone to the wrong place. The old, shoddy-looking site had been replaced by a smooth, clean template design. The link that once read "L.A.M.E! Writers" now said, "About Our Members"—and that section was hardly recognizable. Next to almost every member's name there was now a title: Prince Mishkin was "Director of Operations"; Jolly Jack was "Chief Marketing Officer"; there were now also an Ombudsman, a Public Liaison, a Chief Technologist, and a Public Events Coordinator to deal with.

There were T-shirts for sale, coffee mugs, postcards and key chains, all bearing the L.A.M.E! logo. The crummy, photocopied zines for sale on the site were now being called "exclusive hand-made limited editions" and the prices had all been jacked by a factor of three. There was also a notice for the launch of L.A.M.E! Press: "No manuscript rejected! Once in a lifetime opportunity! National sales force! Anticipated sales of 10,000 L.A.M.E! books by end of summer! Print on demand is the publishing revolution! Don't delay! Send your manuscript to our Chief Literary Officer today!!!"

I began getting emails, from other members. Intrigue was flying, lines were being drawn. Jolly Jack was on a frantic manuscript grab for his print-on-demand scheme. Other L.A.M.E! members were launching presses, like "Real L.A.M.E! Books" and "Original L.A.M.E! Editions, LLC." The message boards were filling with accusations of rip-offs, espionage, and ominous phrases like "intellectual property."

I wrote to Prince: What the hell was going on? What happened to revolution? Toppling edifices and all of that? What happened to working together? This time, it was nearly two weeks before I got the response:

Thank you for your inquiry. After careful consideration we have decided that your request must be handled by our Chief Marketing Officer. Please keep in mind that in the future we will not be able to answer any inquiries that

have not been sent through our Public Relations Officer.
Your cooperation is appreciated.

Sincerely, Office of the Director

I was still reeling when the electronic bell of my email program rang again. What I found there did not surprise me:

Dan: After careful consideration I've decided not to do the book with you, as Prince informs me that you seem insufficiently supportive of the Cause. Besides, we're talking with some folks at Blue Embryo Press and they've got foreign distribution as well as some movie people on board.

It was signed, "Stan 'The Man' Stanislawski."

I emailed the Webmaster—excuse me, Chief Technologist—and told him to remove my picture and bio. The next day they were gone. As I left the L.A.M.E! website for the last time, I stopped by Prince Mishkin's page for a final look. I read a part of "Destroying The Dandies" that once again seemed indirectly addressed to me:

Say a prayer and fond farewell to the failed ideas of the past! Say good-bye to those poor deluded dandies who do not grasp the L.A.M.E! strategy and vision! Bid adieu to those who think they can achieve anything on their own, without the power of a Group behind them! Speak "adios" to those sad individualists leftover from the last century, living in a fantasy world. And say hello to the Revolution!

I deleted the L.A.M.E! bookmark and closed the browser. I sat for a long time, thinking. Then I opened a new file and began composing a letter to Jerome Soforth Wiggins.

Jam It Good

Donald hated Jamaica. Hated the sound of it, even. He wrote the word again and again in his notebook, varying it each time: Jam Ache Ya. Jah Hate Ya. *Jahateya.* Yes, that was it.

"Don Carlos?" Megan asked again. She called him Don Carlos when she saw him pouting, like now. He didn't respond.

"Don Carlos?"—his last name was Charles—"I'm going to the room for a minute. Can I bring you something on my way back?"

Donald looked down at the empty Red Stripe bottle next to the chair, and gave her a curt nod of his head and continued doodling in the notebook; this time, a crude picture of a cross-eyed Rasta with big spirals for hair and a huge joint in his mouth. Donald didn't look up until Megan was far enough away, and then his eyes followed her with a look of impatient sadness. Why did she have to be so damn nice all the time? Why didn't she tell him to go to hell?

Because they were already there, that's why.

He had to remind himself that he would never have come here if Megan hadn't won the tickets through a lottery at work. He had always suspected the island was a dump, and his suspicions had been vividly confirmed. Bob Marley. Rastafari. One Love. Irie. Bullshit.

From the first it had been a disaster. The plane leaving Kennedy was delayed nearly ten hours because of engine trouble; by the time they pulled away from the gate the whole first day was shot. Worse, it meant enduring the harrowing two-hour cab ride from Sanger airport at night, the driver racing wildly over pitted mountain roads, facing down a barrage of speeding headlights coming through the rain—it had to be raining, of course—the other way. By the time they had gotten to the resort it was well past midnight, and they were both almost delirious from hunger, anxiety, and exhaustion.

The next day the weather was beautiful; they had planned on spending a full day on the beach nearby but the moment they left the grounds they were accosted by one of the buzzing vultures lurking outside the resort walls. This one was a carver. Make beautiful animals, *mon*, genuine Jamaican folk art, only twenty dollars American.

He was tall, skinny, with a mess of dirty dreadlocks and gold teeth, as well as the red, dopey eyes of the drug addict. Donald said no, politely. The man persisted; he was not really asking, Donald realized. The salesmen had snarled, "Give me twenty American. You have twenty American." Donald looked at the products. Flimsy, hastily-done animals: salamanders, giraffes, turtles, not carved so much as hacked with electric hand tools. They were the worst carvings he had ever seen, and Donald told the man so.

More arguing, more persistence. They continued walking to the beach, a threesome now, the trinket man extolling the virtues of his handiwork. As soon as they had reached the sand two more salesmen immediately joined them. After a few more minutes of the same demands for outrageous sums, arguments and denials the other two had gone off. The glassy-eyed trinket salesmen planted himself a few feet away in the shade and began huffing on a giant spliff, sucking the paper dick for every drop of smoke.

They tried to go swimming, but the floor of the inlet was covered in rocks; almost immediately Donald felt something slice into the bottom of his foot. He limped out of the water and looked. It was a good one, about the size of a quarter and angled. It would be bleeding for a while, and walking would be tough for several days.

"God damn it," he said, as Megan walked him back to their towels. "God damn this fucking place."

The trinket salesman tried to offer some brittle, gold-toothed words of sympathy, but he didn't press the issue of the trinkets again. "I'll be around tomorrow, *mon*. You can pay me then, *mon*. And be careful where you step, *mon*." Then he had laughed—a wild, sick laugh—and Donald had given him the finger and limped back to the resort with Megan.

"Here you go, handsome."

Donald looked up and squinted. Megan had returned from the room, wearing a straw sun hat and carrying a bottle of Red Stripe and a paperback book. She put the bottle and the book on the ground next to Donald's chair.

"I brought your book, too, just in case you wanted to read."

"Thank you."

How she took it all in stride, he didn't know. He had heard stories about Jamaica—how once you were there you were basically a prisoner, like Cancun. *Consumertration camps*, he called them. Stupid American college students crammed into overpriced hellholes in places like Negril or Montego Bay, drinking Bud Light and grooving to the Marley tribute bands at Rick's. *All right, people, are you feeling IRIE? I said, are you feeling GOOD VIBRATIONS tonight?! Whoo! Right now it's time to...LIVELY UP YOURSELF!* And the college boys with the backward caps and wraparound shades bounced the drunken co-eds on their shoulders and cheered: *Yaaayyy!*

Treasure Beach had promised to be different. It was in a remote section of the southern shore, a largely agrarian and fishing economy that was hours from any of the tourist traps. And it was different, in fact. Not only were there very few Americans of any sort, but so far the locals had been exceptionally nice. When he had gotten back to the compound with his cut foot Donald had gone to the lady at the front desk for a first aid kit, and she had explained to Donald that the trinket salesmen largely came from Kingston, which was a wicked and evil place, and that the resort couldn't legally keep them off the street, and that she was sorry about that. It was small comfort but it had helped somehow, knowing that the locals felt the same way.

They had been at Jake's for four days now, and had ventured off the grounds only one other time, to go to dinner at a nearby restaurant. The trinket and coconut cake salesmen were gone, but the drug dealers were doing a brisk trade. They were scattered up and down the dark street, making deals with pale, sunken-chested white men in various states of undress. As they passed one such transaction, being conducted openly under the bare streetlamp, Donald had heard the white, an American, say, "Yah mon, one love, mon."

How many of them, Donald wondered, saw the rage, the desperation, the grinning sociopathy behind the drug dealers' eyes? How many could feel the seething hatred as they beat their breast and said their mons and iries and rastafaris, and chanted their ooga-booga nonsense?

Donald looked down at the book. He was reading *Gerald*, by Daphne du Maurier. She was a fine writer. Not even Hitchcock had been able to ruin her work, hard as he tried.

He found his place in the book, began reading, then stopped and looked up at Megan. She was engrossed in a magazine. She had a beautiful profile, lounging in her tiny striped bikini that showed off her body so well, the big straw hat tilted down as she read articles like "How To Improve Your Love Life" and "Ten Tips For Better Boobs." That's how they do it, he thought. They read those damn magazines and it turns them into some kind of weird geniuses.

"Thanks for remembering the book," he said to her. "And thanks again for the beer."

Megan looked up, then smiled. "What? Oh, sure, honey. My pleasure."

They both went back to reading, but it was hard for Donald to focus on the words. He kept thinking of the trinket salesman, and his evil red eyes and gold teeth, and his hollow, lifeless laughter. Next time we'll go to the Virgin Islands, he thought, or maybe Key West. He thought of that time in St. Thomas, almost ten years earlier. The two girls he was with had smuggled in some coke, and they had all gone skinny-dipping late, and when he woke up he learned that the girls had both wanted to do a three-way with him, but he was passed out drunk. The opportunity never presented itself again. They were a couple of beauties, too; he wondered what had become of them.

The sun overhead was bright and burning, and the waves splashed against the sea wall below. His foot throbbed where a dirty bandage still covered the wound. Donald took a swig of beer and tried to settle back into the book. He noticed a mosquito on his shin, rubbing its dirty little legs together in preparation, and very carefully he maneuvered the book into position and then slammed it down on his leg. He pried the book away, slowly. He missed.

Anabel

An Unreal Vision of You and I at a Volunteer Fireman Block
Party Somewhere on Long Island:
I keep hearing the Pogues, playing over a p.a. system. The
kids are running around, screaming and laughing. Someone's
making a joke about that mustache I grew a few months back then
quickly shaved off. You and I make eye contact over our paper
plates with the mayo-saturated potato salad and grilled hot dogs.
We pause and smile and this is what our eyes say:
— the potato salad is awful, but we'll eat it anyway,
  because Johnnie's wife made it; and
— we love each other more than two people ever
  have, or will.
Our gaze is broken by the crying of our little girl, who has
tripped and skinned her knee. She's hysterical but she'll live,
we've been through this before. I pick her up and examine the
wound with the utmost gravity, offering smooth assurances, as one
of the guys brings out the firehouse first aid kit. There is such a

big fuss made over her wound that our angel soon forgets her tears and in five minutes is running over to the other kids to show off her bandage. Her younger brother feigns indifference but he can't completely hide his envy, or the fact that he's relieved she's all right.

I do not want this feeling, these thoughts. These are the things I have done, in order: quit drinking; lost God; stopped playing guitar; changed jobs; got married; joined a gym; started drinking; quit the gym; got separated; found God; quit drinking; moved; started playing guitar; got a new job; started drinking; joined another gym—and that's just what I remember.

Do you remember how we met? It was that Halloween party in Brooklyn. It was rainy, and cold, and I saw you leaning against the kitchen wall, like you had been waiting for me. I felt goofy, I had a corduroy jacket and an ugly shirt on, but I didn't care, I really just needed to get out. My confidence level must have been high that night, because later you told me it was my smile that won you over, and the way my teeth looked I almost never smiled. It turned out I had heard your band's demo tape and loved it, I knew every song by heart. We knew some of the same people, small world, ha ha. You had white spots on your front teeth, a bump in your nose, and a weak eye that drifted off from time to time. The way you spoke it sounded like you were always stuffed up. You were perfect.

It's funny, how when I close my eyes and think of my heart—I swear this is true—I see a guy dressed in a heart suit, like one of those big fruits from the underwear commercials, except it's really my heart and he's this big goofball in a red heart suit. His right arm is extended and curved, and he's looking at the empty semicircle of his arm, smiling but confused too, like he can't figure it out. Like it's a bad joke he needs someone to explain to him.

157

It wasn't our fault. There was nothing we could have done. The doctor said it wasn't all that uncommon, and we were lucky we brought you in when we did, because any longer and you might have died. Later on you told me that for a minute you thought you didn't want it anyway, and how bad that made you feel later on. That was the beginning of the end for us, we never even spoke about it again. Even when you had all that pain, that terrible pain for months afterwards that sometimes made me clutch my own stomach in sympathy, we didn't talk about it. And every night I would try to soothe you and say I'm sorry, I'm sorry, I'm sorry.

Our girl would have been 7 this year. In my dreams I call her Anabel.

UNDIE PRESS

Printed in the United States
87837LV00002B/408/A